LOW

Low

JEET THAYIL

FABER & FABER

First published in the USA in 2020
by Faber & Faber Limited
Bloomsbury House
74–77 Great Russell Street
London WC1B 3DA

First published in the UK in 2020

Typeset by Faber & Faber Limited
Printed in the UK by CPI Group (UK) Ltd, Croydon CR0 4YY

We are grateful to the following for permission to reproduce copyright material:

An excerpt from the poem 'An Exequy' by Peter Porter, from *The Cost of Seriousness*, Oxford
University Press, 1978. Reproduced by permission of the Estate of the author; An excerpt
from the poem 'Wanting to Die' by Anne Sexton, from *The Complete Poems by Anne Sexton*,
Houghton Mifflin, 1999, copyright © Linda Gray Sexton and Loring Conant, Jr. 1981.
Reprinted by permission of SLL/Sterling Lord Literistic, Inc., and Lyrics from "The Living
End" written by James McLeish Reid and William Adam Reid. Reproduced courtesy of
Domino Publishing Company Limited.

A CIP record for this book
is available from the British Library

ISBN 978-0-571-36072-7

2 4 6 8 10 9 7 5 3 1

To SB

Though you are five months dead, I see
You in guilt's iconography,
Dear Wife, lost beast, beleaguered child,
The stranded monster with the mild
Appearance, whom small waves tease.

PETER PORTER, *from* 'An Exequy'

Death's a sad Bone; bruised, you'd say,
and yet she waits for me, year after year,
to so delicately undo an old wound,
to empty my breath from its bad prison.

ANNE SEXTON, *from* 'Wanting to Die'

CHAPTER ONE

From the window of the aircraft Dominic Ullis saw a gleaming slum of tin and tarpaulin, close enough to touch. Patchwork shacks crawled downhill, the blue roofs weighted with rocks. The shanty town came right up to the edge of the runway and the plane seemed to skim the houses as it landed.

Too quickly, the wheels hit the tarmac and the woman to his left got up. Because they were in the front row within knee-touching distance of the flight attendants, she was told to sit down and refasten her seatbelt.

She'd boarded late, without hurry, wearing a starched sari and heavy jewellery, hair so silver it might have been dyed.

"I'm Payal," she'd said, taking charge.

"Ullis," he'd replied, his voice rusty with disuse, his name sounding strange to his ears.

"Ulysses," she whispered, pointing at the window, "I think that's my seat." He got up to let her in.

The Ambien bloomed soon after take-off, all twenty milligrams at once. His eyes had closed for a few minutes and for a few minutes he enjoyed his first hit of unconsciousness in days, interrupted only once, by a voice asking if he preferred coffee or tea. Wine, he replied truthfully, wondering where he was (from the window a glimpse of a bright unfamiliar highway dotted with clouds, washed blue prairies without cars or houses). Then his eyes had closed again. He woke to a cleared tray and Payal putting his cutlery into her enormous handbag. She also took her own cutlery and both their headphones and the in-flight magazine.

"You don't mind, do you," she said, seeing he was awake.

"Not at all," he'd managed to mumble. "Be my guest."

The mysterious quality of in-flight air. The low whine of tinnitus, a charged anxious ringing that kept adjusting its volume. The sense of something about to happen, something decisive. Then the lights dimmed as the aircraft dropped through the clouds and prepared to land. It taxied and turned, taxied and stopped.

Payal sprang up again, grabbed her wheeled case from the overhead bin, and went to the front exit, resplendent in her sari. Ullis stayed where he was until the other passengers had left. Then he put half an Ambien under his tongue and took the white plastic box from the overhead bin and floated towards the lovely slum city.

He'd left Delhi on a whim, carrying only the box from the crematorium. If not for the box what would he do with his hands? He would wring them. Repeatedly. Aki was dead and he didn't know what to do from one moment to the next. The vast abstraction of time reduced to this: stupefaction with the hands. For now it was okay. For now his hands were cradling the box that contained her ashes.

The events of the week had passed through him without resistance from the moment he came home to find Aki dead in the study. He'd panicked and called her mother. Then he drove to her house, breathless and shouting in the suffocating car. Aki's mother had come back with him to the apartment in Defence Colony and they'd taken his wife's body to the hospital. A quartet of stone-faced orderlies had moved her from the emergency room to the morgue. All night the panic sat like a heavy bear on his chest. The bear stayed for many days and nights, until it gave way to exhaustion and blessed amnesia. His mind disengaged from his surroundings. He felt separated from his body, but only partially, as if he'd been insufficiently anaesthetised.

Later, the only thing he remembered clearly was the crematorium, the priests in their white dhotis and saffron forehead smears, their oily faces peering at him from clouds of smoke, the cold young eyes devoid of all earthly emotion except boredom. He'd been shaken by their indifference and dazed by all that was expected of him.

Her mother had dressed Aki in a spectacularly inappropriate multi-coloured silk sari, and she'd made Ullis don a black suit and white shirt. He'd added a pair of chocolate loafers for urgent private reasons and foregone a tie as a concession to the April heat. This was how husband and dead wife had arrived at the crematorium: dressed for a wedding, in clothes neither had worn in their life together.

The suit and sari had been unnecessary. There were no mourners, no witnesses other than a handful of crematorium employees and Ullis and his dry-eyed mother-in-law. She had organised the cremation in such haste that there had been no time to call those who had known Aki and loved her. There was no time for anything other than the observance of rituals, each more pointless than the next. The bored priests had mouthed their inane mantras. They had sifted uncooked rice and read from ancient leather-bound tomes and stared with their oily eyes. They rang tiny brass bells in a sequence to which only they were privy. (The bells are an omen, and they ring more than once in this story.) When they demanded of him some minor role in the general pagan tumult, he had obliged with the acquiescence required of the husband of the bride. After all, this was what she had been made to resemble, a young bride in silks and flowers. Except that the marigolds were uniformly wilted. Were they leftovers from a previous funeral?

When the priests told him to push the button that would slide her into the electric furnace, he had worried that the absurd sari would burst into flame. He'd taken a last look at her slight figure dwarfed by piles of flowers and sundry low-priced objects, her face obscured by the sari's pallu, artfully obscured so no viewer would remark at the blood vessels that had burst on her cheeks and forehead and neck like scarlet-brown buds that would never bloom. "Kar do," the priest had said. Obediently Ullis slid her in, and some time later his mother-in-law divided his wife's ashes into two boxes: "One for you and one for me."

From the crematorium, clutching the box and dressed in his mourning suit, he walked into the dust of an enclosed courtyard surrounded by dead trees and broken concrete columns. From there he walked into the dust of the street.

"Dominic," his mother-in-law had said. "You will be all right."

"No," he said. Was she now his *former* mother-in-law?

"Of course you will," she said. "You'll be just fine."

"Okay."

"Shall I ask Jeevan to drop you home?"

"No thank you," he said. "I'll take a taxi."

"Arré, why? I have car and driver. He can drop."

"I'll take a cab. But thanks."

As soon as he took a seat in the back of the battered white Honda that smelled of garam masala and hand sanitiser, Ullis decided not to return to the empty apartment in Defence Colony where each room reminded him of his dead wife and his abject failure as a husband and a man. What was the point of going *home*? It was the last place he wished to go. No, he could do better. He'd travel to a city by the sea. After all, was he not carrying his wife's ashes and did they not need to be immersed?

"Can you take me to the airport?"

The driver was young and easily shocked. He seemed unreasonably upset by the change of plans.

"Sir, I cannot," he said.

"But why not?"

"First, you must change destination on phone."

Ullis opened the app. He deleted 'Defence Colony' from the drop location and typed in 'Delhi Indira Gandhi International Airport'.

In half an hour he was at a reservation desk where he bought himself a ticket to the city he knew best, where oblivion was purchased cheaply and without consequence.

On arrival at the airport in Bombay, Dominic Ullis bought bottled water and took the other half of the Ambien. He swam dreamily through scenes of underwater retail, discount bullion, special offer shipwrecks, select garments for the life aquatic, water-resistant electronics for the discerning pirate, gift shop seashell key-chains and conch paperweights, endless counters of victuals from the ocean featuring sample plates of octopus and oyster and urchin. The water was clean but above him a floating island of garbage had flickered into view. The water was unclean and warming, getting warmer by the minute, so hot his skin was beginning to pucker.

He surfaced from the dream in a taxi. They were nearing a dwarf skyscraper on which had been painted the distorted features of a Bollywood actor, a giant face that flickered and melted and remade itself across a dozen floors as a bloated blond visage, the goofily grinning President of the United States. He was making a speech of some sort, a long, perfectly timed monologue. Not a word of it was true. He was goofily laughing at everyone, most of all the people who took him seriously. He was enjoying himself so much, telling cruel jokes and inventing nicknames. Everything he did was a satire of itself, a satire of presidential gravitas, a satire of compassion and grievance, a satire of civility, masculinity and patriotism. This is why the president was a comfort and an inspiration. It was thrilling to know that nothing was true and therefore everything was true. Everything was true and everything was permitted. The president was living proof that you could say anything and it didn't matter. Communication was concealment. Any kind of unusual behaviour was acceptable as long as you did it often enough. But Ullis couldn't understand why the American president's face was plastered across a low-rise building in Bandra. Was it a workaday Ambien-induced hallucination or the latest advance in digital advertising? Or grief made plain as the inability to trust one's eyes? And while he was taking questions: Where was his luggage? Had he left it on the carousel at the airport?

"Stop, stop," he told the driver. Chewing on gutka, his eyes wild, the driver braked hard and the car skewed to the side of the highway. Ullis got out and found his phone. Then he remembered: he had no luggage. He had no possessions except the cuboid box filled with textured whitish ash. He returned to the taxi's collapsed back seat.

"Aap theek hai, boss?" said the driver as he put the car into gear.

"Hah, theek hai," said Ullis, "sorry."

They bounced towards the smudged horizon. He saw the tollbooths leading to the Sea Link and its quick run to South Bombay. There was a smell of salt and mangrove and deep-sea mud, as if the underwater world he had imagined had begun to seep in through the windows.

"Dekh," said the driver, indicating the sea that had come into view. Seen from a distance it was clean, blue-green, untouched by the city's chemical overflow. "Over there? Statue of Shivaji Maharaj is coming, biggest in whole world, Shivaji and horse in the middle of Arabian Sea."

"Acha?"

"Kyon? Hum bhi kissise kum nahin."

"First class," said Ullis. "Absolutely deadly."

"Ji," said the driver. "First class!"

It appeared that the city's long-drawn burial rite was reaching its end stage with a final display of extravagance and splendid insanity. This much was certain: the statue's completion and its annihilation would occur simultaneously. As the Doomsday Glacier dissolved and the oceans grew, only the tip of the statue's ceremonial sword would be seen, for a moment, before that too went under. The city would be swallowed alive. Why judge or decry any of it? Perhaps the world's tallest statue would provide succour to the damned. Perhaps a drowned monument to a long-dead warrior was as important as higher ground or shelter from the storm. It was possible. Anything was possible at the end of days.

"Bandra," he said, as calmly as he could. "Left lena, please."

"Left?" asked the cabbie, unfazed. To their left was the glittering expanse of the sea.

"Nahi, right," said Ullis apologetically. "Right lena."

The cabbie found his last packet of gutka and tore the silver foil with his teeth and poured the contents into his mouth. He resolved to buy more when the crazy passenger had left the cab. He'd been driving since Thursday night and now it was Friday and he hadn't slept or changed his clothes or been to the toilet. He knew that without the gutka he would not be able to drive or think. Perhaps he should recommend it to the passenger? It was obvious the man needed a cure for whatever ailment he was suffering from. Gutka was reliable in the way it focused the mind, especially if the mind was fractured. As the sick-sweet smell of tobacco and lime spread into the car, the driver glanced in the rear-view at the passenger with no luggage who had asked him to stop the cab for no reason. The man had fallen asleep clutching his box. They had reached Bandra, but where in Bandra did he want to go? At Carter Road the exhausted cabbie parked near a tender coconut stand and wound down his window and let the sea breeze fill the car.

When Ullis awoke from a less-than-refreshing narcotic-induced interlude, it was dark. The driver was stretched out in the front seat. To his left the sea was a hanging mess of mangroves under a sky the colour of dirty pewter. Crowds of people massed on the promenade. The car smelled terrible, the usual smell of sea and sewage plus the clotted emanations of two sleeping men. Gently he tried to wake the driver. "Excuse me, driver-ji," he said, tapping the man on the shoulder. There was no response. He got out of the car and put some money on the dashboard and set off towards Pali Hill. Inevitably he tripped over a small pyramid of coconuts and fell noisily to his knees. Somehow, with a complex system of fumbles, he managed to save the white box and its precious cargo.

On he plodded, stumbling slightly past an ornate white cross, one of several hundred in the neighbourhood. He passed a patch of undeveloped ground in which the rusted skeleton of a once-yellow school bus had grown into the soil like a prehistoric burial site. He knew now where he was going – the bungalow his friend Neel had converted into a cafe – and he was happy to let his feet lead him. A sound general rule: follow the feet rather than the head. There was less chance of being led astray. As he neared the cafe he saw a figure in cargo shorts and T-shirt, the default uniform of the Bandra man. It was Neel, staring at the endless traffic.

By way of greeting he said, "What are you doing in Bombay? What's with the suit?"

The smile disappeared as it came to him.

"Christ," he said, "I'm so sorry about Aki. It must be the worst time."

Ullis considered this. "As bad as it's ever been," he agreed.

"Fair enough," said Neel.

"Or ever will."

"Let's go in for a minute, sit down. It's good to see you. I mean it, welcome home. It's still home, isn't it, even if you've been away so long?"

"Home," said Ullis, as his mind blanked on the meaning of the word.

"How long?"

He had no idea. He only knew it had been years. Once he had been cursed with memory. Now he had the gift of forgetting. And anyway, what difference? From now on, time was divided into

9

before Aki and after. Only the years in between had any historical shape or density.

"Ten," said his friend. "Ten years. You were here right up until 2008 in that little studio down on Carter Road. Then you moved to New York and married Aki and everybody thought that was that, you'd never come back."

"Right," said Ullis. It *had* been the plan, to not come back. But one morning, naked on the velvet two-seater that served as their couch, Aki had come up with the idea that changed everything: *We should go back to India, live small, write a book.* And here he was, in India without her, coming apart in slow motion. Clearly, fortification was needed. Pupils dilating in anticipation, he said: "Shall we get some red wine? I've got a long-standing craving."

"How are you holding up? You're not looking so great, to tell you the truth. Not great and not good. Listen, I'm so sorry about Aki."

"Thanks," said Ullis, consolingly. Then: "Let's find a bottle of red."

The cafe had no liquor licence but they would drink the wine out of coffee cups. Neel called Pinky Wines down the road. A delivery was accepted, the delivery man tipped, the bottle in its black plastic bag opened, the wine poured and half of it drunk, in minutes; and soon they were joined by familiar faces from the Bombay night whose names he was unable to remember, whose faces he recalled but only because they had shared the fourth watch for many nights over many months and years. Nothing had changed. The same people saying the same things, the same lies and boasts, the insults and gossip, the overriding need to postpone the moment when it was time to go home.

Around him the voices swirled.

"People like meow because it's cheap."

"How cheap is cheap?"

"A thousand a gram?"

"I asked him what his safe word was and he was like, *Ouch*."

"Is that Amitabh Bachchan?"

"Of course not, it's his stunt double. See the hair? Real!"

"Then I said, *Don't you wanna know mine?* He said, *Sure I do.* And I said, *Don't stop*."

"Telling you. You have to pay me to do a drug called meow meow. What's next, woof woof?"

At least nobody laughed. Ullis dug into his pockets to check how much cash he was carrying, and thought: I don't mind a joke, no, a joke is acceptable, what I object to is the laughter, forced or maniacal, by which it is followed.

"It's not so bad, except for the crash. Sussidal."

"Uh, no? No. No. No."

"Oh yeah it is. I see those people? I'm, like, legit creeped out, baby. The lights are on and nobody's home."

"Ketamine's an animal sedative. It was never meant for humans. Why would you take it if you're not a horse?"

"Right, stick to cocaine! Stick to molly!"

"Who said we're human?"

"I'm sticking to meow."

"So bonkers, you guys and your bonkers consumerism. Drug users are the ultimate consumers, spend all your money on stuff that's gone in a day. Wake up and do it again."

"Sorry, do you know where I can get some?"

Ullis heard the flat, hesitant tone in which the last question was asked and recognised the voice as his own.

Surprised, guilty and vaguely resentful to be alive, Dominic Ullis woke on a couch in the morning glare, no more suicidal than usual. Where was the crash he'd been promised? All around him men and women lay on the floor in unnatural poses, as if an airborne virus had felled them where they stood. He was in Bandra possibly, because there were palm trees outside the window. How had he got into the city from the airport? What happened afterwards? He recalled very little after leaving the crematorium, when was it, yesterday or the day before? The realisation that he retained no sense of the recent past gave him an immediate sense of wellbeing. All hail prescription meds, he murmured to the sleeping horde, all hail the wide umbrella of the narcotic.

He went into the next room where more people were asleep or passed out. A couple sat cross-legged on the floor. The guy was making lines on a mirror he had taken off the wall. A dusty rectangle marked the spot. When he saw Ullis he said: "Not again. Man, you're insatiable!" Ullis nodded politely, though he had no idea what the guy was talking about. The girl held out a straw. He snorted a fat line of the chalky beige powder, which burned his nostrils and broke his vision into slices and lowered him to the ground. Into a corner he slumped. His heart raced and his nerves vibrated with a jumpy premonition. Here was none of the cool measured anxiety of cocaine. No false and pleasurable clarity, only disconnection and faint nausea. He took a moment to enjoy the different flavours that dripped into the back of his throat, the powdered milk, the animal tranquilliser, the chemicals and secret compounds he couldn't identify. They made more lines until the bag was finished. At some point he found himself searching the tiled floor for granules that might have fallen into the cracks. He was rewarded with a speck that might or might not have been meow meow. He put it on his tongue.

He had a sudden vision of the tarpaulin-covered shacks that surrounded the airport in Bombay, the slum-dwellers swarming like ants on a mountain of black sugar, children at play in the sewage and waving at the plane overhead, mothers tending cook fires on the landfill, washing hung to dry on roofs and doors and nails. A republic of the dispossessed in service to those who lived in the tall blocks that pockmarked the city, where everything was true and everything was permitted. He was as much a member of the republic as anyone.

On his tongue the meow was serum: there is no truth but the rush, there is no rush but the truth of your senses. Come to me, oh captain, my Captain Meow, lead me to the light.

Minutes or hours later, he left the apartment and walked three floors down to the street. There he stopped. Briskly, efficiently, he went back up the stairs and rang the bell. The couple let him in. He found the white box on the floor under the couch on which he'd passed out.

"What's in the box?" said the girl.

"My wife," said Ullis.

"Your wife. Is she dead?"

"Of course she's dead," said the guy. "Come on, even I know that and I'm not even a graduate."

"How did she die?" said the girl.

"Her heart stopped," said Ullis, making his standard reply. In a way it was true: when a person dies their heart stops.

"Where did it happen?"

"In the study," said Ullis. This at least was entirely true.

"Where were you?"

"Out. I came home and found her."

"When was this?" said the girl.

"Around midnight on the first of April," he said. "Any more questions? You might as well get it over with."

"What was COD?"

"Pardon me?"

"Cause of death, what was cause of death?"

"She made a mistake," he said, wondering if by some chance the girl had intuited the truth. "No, I made a mistake. *I'm* the mistake, *me*. I should have stayed home."

"I'm sorry," she said.

"I'm sorry too, bra," said the guy. "I mean, that has to be the worst April Fool's joke of all time."

"My name's Amrut," said the girl, "and this is Sriram. We're going out for breakfast. Want to come?"

He didn't hesitate.

He said: "I don't see why not."

CHAPTER TWO

They walked two long blocks to 14th Road, to a doctor's clinic on the ground floor of a residential building. A tanker parked in front of the gate spilled great splashes of water from its open spout, and a wet trail stretched all the way to the end of the street and beyond. Dominic Ullis stared at the spreading puddle and realised that he'd never seen a water tanker in an Indian city that did not spill its resource on the streets. He tried (unsuccessfully) to skirt the rust-coloured water body, lifting his feet and bringing them down in an ungainly new dance. But in minutes the water had engulfed his chocolate loafers. Frowning in disbelief at his prized footwear – the loafers concerning which his wife had made her opinion abundantly clear, the very loafers that soon would be engulfed in a more revolting material than dirty water – he thought about the Great Drought. Everybody knew it was coming but what difference did the knowledge make? Perhaps indifference *was* the correct response to cataclysm.

"If you live like there's no tomorrow, there's no tomorrow," he muttered to his new friends.

"Breakfast of champions," said Amrut brightly, pushing open the door to the clinic. "Trust me, it will change your day if not your whole life, starting now."

"For the better, I hope," Ullis said.

It was early and the office was empty. Amrut gave the receptionist their names and eyed the elderly armchairs that lined the waiting room. They sank into the only couch, a beat-up three-seater that may not have seen better days. On the opposite wall was a framed poster of footprints on a beach at sunset, the words *Nothing gold can stay* inscribed in cursive across a cloudless sky.

Ullis wasn't surprised to find an unattributed Robert Frost fragment in the waiting room of a suburban Bombay mounte-bank, but why this fragment in particular? In the context of a doctor's office it may have been intended as a comment on the body as the locus both of Eden and the Fall of Man, the body as the original felix culpa, the happy fault and happier fall. In its current state his body was the site of a double jackpot: memory that was partial and forgetfulness that was complete. Was there a name for his condition, in which he recalled events from the distant past but could not remember what had happened yesterday or even this morning? Was forgetfulness a function of grief? If so it was a blessing, a biological corrective. Forget everything! It will do you good. Forgetfulness as an evolution-ary tool, auto-diagnosis as self-healing. If there was such a thing as healing – at the moment it didn't seem possible. The only thing possible now was oblivion, with the aid of certain pow-dery or liquid substances.

He took out his phone and square-formatted the camera and took a quick photo of the offending poster. He was going to keep a Record of Things. (The resolution slipped his mind in all of two minutes when he saw a WhatsApp forward that suggested the American president would not last his full term, an idea that left him newly bereft, lonelier than ever and afraid for the future.)

"Patience, you need a lot of it in a doctor's office. That's why they call us patients, am I right?" said Amrut. There was no response from her companions. She continued, "And why do they make us wait anyway, doctors? It's a power trip, right?"

"Obvious," said Sriram. He had a rounded rough-hewn face that dropped easily into a smile. He smiled a lot, but there was something about it that felt off, dangerous, a warning of some sort.

"I bet he's in there watching cat videos on Twitter," Amrut said. "They make you wait and wait and then they give you drugs in exchange for money. They're like dealers, dude."

She settled into the couch and crossed her arms and imagined a gold lamé sari dress that could be worn with the pallu draped around the neck like a halter, like a *gold stay*. She imagined a collection of gold saris made of chiffon and georgette silk like the saris worn by Bollywood starlets of the seventies, those vanished girls who went by one name, Mumtaz or Dimple or Helen. She would call the collection *Nothing Gold Can Stay* and the models would walk the ramp in gold sneakers and blonde wigs. Everything would be gold, the catwalk, the make-up, the jewellery and accessories, everything: gold and properly expensive. The dress code would be gold on gold with a touch, just a suggestion, of black. For theme music she would play Shirley Bassey's 'Goldfinger' followed by David Bowie's 'Golden Years' and Golden Earring's 'Radar Love'. Bombay's lunching ladies would eat it up.

Sriram read it twice, *Nothing gold can stay*. He knew it was absolutely, inarguably true. And it was an invitation to mayhem, a come-hither to the reaper of souls, the fearsome one resplendent in his gold chains and blue-black skin, the one who rode a great black buffalo, noose in one hand and danda in the other. If gold cannot stay it meant the soul reaper was on his way. But Sriram would not take fright at such a vision. If anything, it made him want to take his fate into his own hands. Not with drugs, no, that was a flawed cliché. Pointless. Cowardly. He didn't want to die with his senses dulled. He wanted to feel everything. Plan it carefully and time it right. Next month, when Amrut went to New York to visit her parents and his own parents would be in Mysore tending to the family farm, then, on his own terms, alone at home, conscious and aware, certain beyond doubt that gold cannot stay because only the gold die young.

"The doctor will see you now," said the receptionist. She took Amrut and Sriram into a shared examination room. Ullis was shown into an adjoining cubicle. He was told to lie down by a man sporting blue jeans and a blue denim shirt open to the sternum. A golden Om symbol nestled against grey chest hair. He put a towel on Ullis's chest and asked him to remove his dark glasses.

"Are you the doctor?" Ullis asked.

"*Hah!*" the man said, smiling, pleased to be mistaken for his boss. "Doctor is coming. You may put your package there, on the counter. Now please to wait."

Unpleased, Dominic Ullis handed over his white box and waited. And waited. Much later, a man came in wearing a mask and apron. Nothing could be seen of his face except pop eyes behind thick glasses. He switched on an overhead lamp that threw horror movie shadows on the walls. For a wild moment, Ullis considered bolting before the man in the mask unveiled a Judas cradle or iron maiden, some dread instrument of medieval torture. But flight would be tricky: the assistant in the Canadian tuxedo stood guard at the door. At least Ullis wasn't strapped to the chair. If things got hairy he was always at liberty to resist.

"And how are we today?"

"Just peachy," said Ullis, whose wit did not find its true métier with doctors and counsellors and therapists. How well could you be in a doctor's office, at the mercy of a man with a mask and a questionable manner? You weren't on a social call.

"Any blood disorders or allergies?"

"Are you the doctor?" said Ullis. "I'd like a reference point."

The man pointed to a framed certificate that hung beside a fire extinguisher. Ullis made out tiny print and a signature at the bottom right. For all he knew, it was a diploma from an agricultural college or veterinary school or a correspondence course in homeopathy.

"Allergies?" said the man in the mask. "Disorders?"

"Only insomnia and anxiety."

"No worries then. Who doesn't have those things? Is there any medical history I *should* know about?"

"I have hepatitis C."

"Ah yes, very nice, and how did you get it if you don't mind me asking?"

"I shared needles in my youth."

"A fun-filled youth, I'm guessing?"

"Anything but."

"Well, let me assure you that here we don't share needles. You may put your mind at ease."

He said something inaudible to the man in denim and denim, who went off to rummage in what Ullis assumed was the medicine cabinet.

"Right-o, where do you want it?"

"Sorry, what?" said Ullis. What on earth was the old quack quacking on about?

"The injection," said the doctor, making a pumping motion with his thumb and two fingers, "where do you want it?"

"What are the options?"

"Bicep or bum."

"Bicep, thanks very much."

The assistant gave the doctor a filled syringe. When the doctor approached, Ullis got a whiff of his aftershave – eau d'overpowering. Then the man pinched a piece of Ullis's shoulder and threw the needle in like a dart and pressed the plunger. The pain was sharp and satisfying. He was good to go except for the obvious question.

"What was in the shot?"

"Vitamin B12," said the man, removing his mask. "You mean you didn't know?"

"I had no idea."

The doctor blinked owlishly behind his glasses. He had shaved badly. Errant whiskers sprouted in a red patch on his neck. He smelled of fenugreek and asafoetida from the idlis and sambar he had eaten for breakfast. Ullis tried not to gag.

"I can see you are the aficionado of needles," said the doctor. Ullis noticed that he had used eyeliner or kajal. "I can think of no other reason someone would voluntarily choose a blind shot so early in the morning."

Dominic Ullis massaged his punctured bicep and allowed that there was some truth to the doctor's uninformed diagnosis. He had attempted many kinds of rehab and detox over two decades of heroin use. Nothing had worked. In New York he joined a methadone programme designed to get heroin addicts off the street and keep them dependent on cheap government-subsidised opiates.

(He weaned himself off the methadone too, by slowly and methodically reducing his dosage. It took a year and a half, a gruelling time that cured him of the heroin hunger for ever. Or almost for ever.) At the clinic they made him take routine tests for the Aids and hepatitis C viruses. One came back positive. He was sent to the resident doctor who eagerly, too eagerly, recommended interferon, used with varying degrees of success on hepatitis C sufferers. It was a kind of chemotherapy and the side effects were severe, the doctor cheerfully told him. But the alternative was liver cancer and cirrhosis.

"And let me just say that cirrhosis is not the ideal end to your days," said Dr Benedicte S. Bratt, for that was the name on the nameplate.

Imagine Dominic Ullis's response to this prognosis. Imagine his new appreciation for the heavy-handedness of metaphor and the symmetry of fate: a course of forced injections for one who'd been forced to deny the pleasure of the needle's bite and ejaculate.

"Where are you from?" the methadone doctor had said with a winning smile.

"India," said Ullis.

"Ah," said the doctor. "I've heard that Indian tap water must be brought to a roiling boil for twenty minutes to kill viruses, bacteria and other pathogens. Is this generally true?"

"I have no doubt it most probably is generally true."

"Of course, Indians have no trouble drinking their water. They drink it quite happily. It's us foreigners who get sick," said Dr Bratt helpfully. "By the by, roiling does not necessarily kill a virus. It only renders it temporarily inactive."

Ullis wondered if the doctor was referring to all viruses or only the pesky Indian virus.

"Or," said Ullis, "instead of roiling and boiling you could try filtered water."

"You could, but what's the point? No amount of filtration or boiling helps if the water is toxic with pesticides and chemicals to begin with," said the doctor, deploying his sunny smile. "I hear this too can be a problem in India."

"I'm pretty sure you're probably right," said Ullis. "You seem to know a lot about India. Have you been there?"

"Good heavens no," said Dr Bratt as the smile left his face. "I'm not insane, you know."

"No," said Ullis. "Surely not."

"Do you have family in New York or elsewhere in the contiguous United States?" Dr Bratt clicked a plastic ballpoint pen with his thumb. He positioned his fist over a stained yellow pad as if readying to punch Ullis in the eye.

"No," said Ullis truthfully. He had no family in the United States: he had not yet met Aki.

"Ah," Dr Bratt said again, licking chapped lips. "May I make a suggestion?"

"Of course, doctor," said Ullis.

"I happen to know that clinical trials are in progress for a new drug," Dr Bratt said, sniffing delicately. His voice had dropped by several notches. "I am in the position of being able to offer you a place in the final run of trials. I'm happy to announce that we are very close to finding a cure to this tragic disease. It will cost you nothing. A course of medication over a few months and hey presto, Bob's your uncle."

"He's not."

"Sorry?"

"He's not my uncle."

"Oh," said Dr Bratt, "ha ha, no, except in a manner of speaking. Just something we say here in America. You should think it over. Today may be the luckiest day of your life."

Ullis thought it over. Why not? He had nothing to lose. Either he would be cured or he would stay viral. Either he would get better or he would stay the same. There really wasn't much to think about. Except that his viral load had not reached an impasse. Why cure something that had not yet become fatal? Why fix something that was still only life threatening, that hadn't yet become life taking?

"I've thought about it," he said. "I think not."

"But why not," said the doctor, his fist ready to punch or to scribble. "Think about it some more. Weigh your options, fella. It won't cost you a penny. I tell you what, when this drug comes to market it'll be practically unaffordable for someone with a pre-existing condition. I'm afraid hepatitis C qualifies as exactly that."

Ullis thought about it some more. He weighed his options. It took all of three seconds. He was always happy to postpone the unpleasant inevitable. Why do today what could be put off until tomorrow?

"I have a question for you," he said in as casual a manner as possible. "How much time do I have?"

Dr Bratt threw his pen on the pad. He rubbed his stubble with both hands. Ullis noticed that the doctor had missing lashes and missing eyebrows and a possibly compensatory walrus moustache.

"The question is," said Dr Bratt, dazzling smile back in place, "does the virus have a life of its own, or does it exist solely because of a host, which in this case is you, my friend? My own opinion is rooted in daily interactions with host organisms such as yourself. The virus has existed longer than other life forms, certainly longer than humanoid forms. Without cellular structure or a metabolic existence, how does it proliferate? Is it in fact an alien life form that inhabits host structures, human, animal and plant, while it finds ways to evolve and replicate as efficiently as possible? This is the question you must ask yourself."

Ullis suddenly became aware of the doctor's odd taste in decor. Sketches of H. R. Giger's reptilian humanoid monsters adorned the walls. On the desk was a still from *Alien* in which the salivating monster's wide-open mouth tried to kiss or eat the terrified Sigourney Weaver. In a corner between two bookshelves was a life-size replica of the wide-skulled alien. The serrated tail was the size of a small car.

In a way, it explained the doctor's manner with the junkies and former junkies who came to him with their doomed medical predicaments. To him they were aliens he was forced to nurse. Who knew what kind of disappointment he was subject to? Who could blame him for dismissing his patients as statistics, guinea pigs, hosts to an alien virus? Who could blame him for classifying them as carriers of self-inflicted poison, death addicts marking their last moments on earth? There was hardly any point trying to cure them when most often they relapsed or succumbed to some opportune infection. No wonder he chose to amuse himself. Rather than offer practical advice that in any case would be ignored, he preferred to give lessons in abstraction. Particularly when the patient was not amenable to sense and had no wish to be part of a trial that would change the course of medical history and put Dr Benedicte S. Bratt's name among the pioneers of modern viral research.

"This is riveting, don't get me wrong," Ullis said. "But I'm interested in knowing how long I have before the cirrhosis sets in?"

"I believe viruses are found wherever life is found. The two thousand plus viruses discovered to date are only a fraction of the number extant on the planet. I believe, further, that they are descended from a common ancestor and this ancestor is a humanoid, not a viroid life form. In other words it is not a battle we are engaged in, human against virus, as much as a form of co-existence. Oh, but to answer your banal question, I'd say you have until about 2010."

A week after this terrible prophecy, he met Aki on a Saturday afternoon when he was the only occupant of the university library's study room. (More about this meeting in a later chapter. For now let's say that Mexican food was as important an element as Bob Dylan.) She buzzed from the street and he let her in. In four months they would be married, a connection that began when he asked her to the Dylan concert at Madison Square Garden. They smoked a joint before the show. The singer had become old and ornery. He produced a perfectly adequate hour and a half of music backed by a perfectly adequate group of musicians. Hidden under a cowboy hat, he stood towards the back of the stage like a session musician hired for the night. He did not say a word to the audience, not *good evening* or *thank you* or *what's up, New York?* He didn't ask if they were having a good time. He enacted his songs coldly and efficiently and played an encore and left the stage. Ullis had admired his workmanlike demeanour and been outraged by his indifference. Aki was quiet all evening. She told him months later that she agreed to go only because he'd been so enthusiastic. To her the man on stage was an old crooner whose time had a-changed. She preferred female singers, particularly non-white singers of dubious sexual orientation.

Afterwards they walked downtown. The city seemed oddly deserted for a weekend. They passed town houses and a small church. It was late and the temperature had dropped. There was a smell of exhaust fumes and Indian food. He tried to read the expression on her face, but she used her hair to hide her eyes and she rarely looked at him directly. She was small and entirely self-contained, impervious to the world and to anything he might say or do.

"I have to tell you something," he had said.

"Sure," said Aki. "Sit here for a minute."

They perched on the steps of the church and watched the sparse late-night traffic hiss past on the street. He told her that in his twenties and thirties in Bombay he had been a user of opium and heroin, that he had contracted an incurable virus and that he did not know how much time he had. Aki listened without comment. After a while she roused herself and said that nobody knew how much time they had. It was something we all had in common. Nobody knows anything, she said, but they pretend they do. They act like they have all the time in the world and they're going to live for ever, which is the worst possible thing to assume. It isn't going to happen. Nobody lives for ever, thank God.

"Every one of us lives with a death sentence," she said.

She said the thing that made him different was that he knew it. He knew the truth, that time was limited and each day you stayed alive you beat the odds just a little. And besides, he seemed perfectly healthy. There was always the possibility that he would live a long life, that he would outlive her, for example.

"I doubt it," Ullis had said, foolishly, stupidly, idiotically.

Aki shrugged exaggeratedly. Then she said she had something to tell him as well, if they were being honest and upfront and all.

It took him a moment to understand what she was saying because an unaccustomed feeling had come to him then, something that might have been happiness. As if he was exactly where he was meant to be, for once, in the right place at the right time. Then he heard her words and the feeling disappeared. He was filled with apprehension.

"Ever since I was little?" she said. "I've wanted to die."

"To die," he said, robotically.

"Yes, it's all I can remember. As I grow older I think about it more and more. I want to die."

She told him that she had felt abandoned as a child because her parents had left her with relatives when she was just three. For years she had lived with aunts and cousins. The early severing had changed her for ever. How had it changed her? For example, fifteen or so years later, she had fallen in love with someone for the first time. When he told her that his family had arranged his marriage to a girl from his hometown, she had accepted it without comment. There was a lot to be done, he told her, all kinds of arrangements had to be made and it was beyond him. He didn't know what to do. Aki said she would help and she did, she helped organise his wedding to another woman. She had never blamed anyone for the things that had happened to her, she said. It was just that sometimes she felt low.

She called it 'the low'. It was the great constant in her life. "I was always able to access the low," she said, as if it were a resource or a country. "I always returned to the low." For example, on the flight from Bombay to New York she had asked for mango juice. The steward told her they were out of mango. Could he bring her something else? She asked for vodka. He came around after he had served the other passengers, and to make up for the delay he brought her two large drinks. She had wanted mango juice and she ended up drinking two double vodkas. Also, it was the first day of her period. She said, "I came down with a heavy case of the low."

Ullis understood in an instant that she was doing what he had done, offered a picture of himself with the drawbacks, which were considerable, placed prominently in the foreground. As if to say, this is what you're in for, if you don't want it say so now.

"It's okay," he'd said.- "We'll help each other stay alive."

And now here was Dominic Ullis, well past his sell-by date, still alive and moderately kicking and stepping out into the sunshine with Amrut and Sriram, while his wife was ashes in a box clutched in his unworthy hands. It was intolerable.

"Wasn't that just the best?" said Sriram.

"Oh, hell yeah," said Amrut. "So are you all pumped up with the bee juice?"

"That's not the word I'd use, exactly."

"Well, I am! Pumped! Ready to start hustling. Like, brace yourself, Bombay! Here I come. How you feeling? Say something."

"Not much different, to tell you the truth, except for the weird chemical smell on my skin."

"Dude," said Amrut, "that isn't the B12, that's the meow. It means the crash is coming, worst crash of your life. Only one way to fight it, isn't that right, Sriram?"

Sriram regarded her with infinite sadness.

"Here," said Amrut, passing something to Ullis, "take this and go to the loo. Just don't finish it, okay?"

She looked at the big white dial of her watch. Already ten. She almost wanted to stick around. She was enjoying this, showing the newbie how to negotiate the byways and highways of meow. But how was it already ten? She had a studio to get to and interns to direct and a whole day to set in motion. She had a meeting in the afternoon with a videographer who would make a short film about her label. Her idea was to use the kind of models rarely seen in Indian advertisements, curvy girls, dark-skinned girls, girls who looked like they worked for a living and didn't mind getting their hands dirty. She had an idea for a one-shot take and she wanted to block it out today, choreograph each element, the costumes, the accessories, the models, the extras, the vehicles, the location, how many crew members they would need, how much time. Accordingly she would fix the budget and run it past her partners, which was always her least favourite part of the business. She would be gone all day. She wouldn't see Sriram again until midnight but she couldn't worry about him now. She had worried about him enough. She had her own problems to fix and her own life to manage.

Ullis palmed the tiny envelope and went to the facilities in the back. They were at the kind of establishment in which he did not trust the drinking water, much less the toilets. Once one of Bombay's beloved Irani restaurants, it had fallen on hard times. The strong milk tea was no longer served in glass tumblers but in thimble-sized plastic cups. Linoleum and benches had replaced the marble-top tables and wooden chairs. The Irani owners were long gone and the restaurant had become the kind of place described by guidebooks as 'shabby' and 'cheap'. Which made it perfect for Ullis's purposes. This morning, cheap and shabby was how he felt.

He found himself in a small room with a commode and no sink. He shut the toilet seat with his shoe and examined and dismissed the top of the water tank. Not wanting to touch anything, he extracted the folded rectangle of paper and dipped in a fingernail and snorted a clot of moist beige powder. He waited a moment and did it again. The burn was a contradictory impulse in his nostrils, a speedy drowsy numbness with no pain. His heart speeded up. Or had it slowed down? Had it sputtered into an arrhythmic skip and tumble? He couldn't tell. It was all so confusing, really. Was he high or low?

When he returned to the table it was spread with dishes, each submerged under a generous layer of golden-brown oil.

"Kheema, egg akuri and brain fry," said Sriram, waving at the victuals, "cutting chai is on the way."

Ullis put a helping of mince on a plate and helped himself to a roti. He took a bite and felt a muscle memory of something that might have been hunger, except that it disappeared almost immediately and was replaced by a moderate wave of nausea. He gave up the attempt at breakfast. Instead he ordered three whiskies and a bucket of ice.

"Bit early in the day, don't you think?" said Amrut, reluctant all of a sudden to drink.

"A medicinal beverage," said Ullis. "At least it will stay down."

When the whisky arrived they clinked glasses. Amrut considered her drink then downed it in a single draught. Sriram dipped his finger in the glass and threw a drop of liquor on the empty chair opposite.

"To our absent chuddy buddies," he said.

The bill arrived and Ullis insisted on paying.

"Least I can do," he said. "And do you mind if I keep the rest of the meow? Here's a thousand with my thanks."

"That's too much, but okay," said Amrut. "Let it never be said that I said no to cash. Right, guys?"

Ullis saw movement on the floor. A small boy who could not have been more than seven or eight pushed a large brown rag sideways and forwards. The rag left circular streaks of wet dirt in its wake, which the boy's bare feet smudged into flower-like patterns of chocolate and gold. The meow, Ullis realised, had a way of accentuating the sordid. A vision of a child labouring in a filthy restaurant, a sight seen across the city a thousand times a minute, acquired the tragic nuance of a nineteenth-century novel. His nausea worsened. He wanted more than anything to be alone in a taxi that would transport him across the Sea Link to southernmost Bombay.

"Well, Amrut," he said, shaking hands, not forgetting to pick up the white box on the bench beside him. "Sriram. It's been a ride. Thank you and may your crashes all be painless."

And he was out. He flagged a black and yellow that took him creakily to the sea. Where would he go? How far was far enough from the breathless suburbs of Bandra?

"Take me to the Taj," he said.

"Kaunsa Taj, bhaiyya?" said the cabbie.

"The real one in Colaba," said Ullis. "Where else?"

"Real one not in Colaba, baba, real one in Agra," said the cabbie, trying to be a smartass.

Ullis put the window down and took a deep breath of the carbon-laden air. It was a mistake. He was caught by a violent fit of coughing. Feeling a little sick, he slouched against the seat and looked up at the ceiling of the cab, which was too low and too close to his face. The padded plastic had a blue-and-copper snakeskin pattern that repeated dizzyingly across the length and breadth of his vision. Rivets splayed dramatically across, grooved like bullets. For some reason the rococo design reminded him of Elvis Presley and deep-fried peanut butter sandwiches, which worsened his nausea.

On the street a homeless woman gesticulated with one arm. With the other she held together the caked and blackened petticoat that served as a skirt. She caught Ullis's eye and laughed. Her red mouth was wet in the streaked dirt of her face.

They passed houses on a hill where the movie stars lived, prime real estate that would be worth nothing as the sea encroached, day by day, year by year, the waters heating and rising. They passed a market and a church where he had once undergone rehab. Part of the recovery regimen had been the cleaning of the church premises once a week. He remembered that he'd enjoyed sweeping the floors and washing the stained glass and wiping down the pews.

And then, in a small storefront that bought old newspapers by the kilo, he seemed to see his wife, stooped and bewildered, watching him go past as if he was someone she recognised but could not remember. As if she longed to go with him if only she could. Her face was unchanged, pale and round, but her hair was cut short and in the bright morning sun the sari she wore was phosphorescent, an emission of light that imprinted itself on his retinas and recurred in flashes as an afterglow.

CHAPTER THREE

In the back of the taxi Ullis sat slumped, remembering blood roses and the taste of her breath as it turned. The driver took the ramp for the Sea Link and stopped the car creakily at a toll-booth. There was a white ship on the water, its top half freshly painted. Red stripes unfurled like ribbons across the bridge. But below the sparkle of the top deck it was unpainted industrial metal, ready for the scrapyard. Like the city, the ship was all facade, a brave offering against the sea, a token structure of resistance, dazed yet hopeful.

"Singul, ya return?" said the cabbie.

"Single," said Ullis, handing over seventy rupees for a one-way ticket. He put earphones in and pressed play on his iPod, and held his breath as Schubert's 'Ave Maria' began and the harped strings of the bridge accelerated above him.

After Aki's death he'd played the song at top volume at all times of day and night. It had helped to still the panic that seeped like smoke inhalation into his chest. Later, other emotions replaced panic, mainly anger and guilt. He came to a decision. He would adopt a bit of practical advice from the handbook of Jean Rhys: drink, drink, drink. As soon as you sober up, you start again. Force it down if you have to. Whatever it may be, vodka, bourbon, wine, meow meow, cocaine, heroin, force it down like medicine. This was his new mission, and he pursued it devotedly. But anxiety always bubbled under, untouched by the ongoing blizzard of alcohol and drugs with which he tried to obliterate it.

Now he let the music do its work. The flattened emotion of the voice and the grave melody were inseparable from suffering yet unmoved by it. He'd always assumed that the singer was Maria Callas. In the story he heard somewhere, she'd recorded the song the year she died from an overdose of Mandrax, a favourite substance of his own youth. (Was there a lovelier word, evoking both Mandrake the comic-strip magician and Mandragora the fabled deliriant – and ending with a final chop of the axe?) 'Ave Maria' was one of the first pieces of music he had given Aki, who looked it up and discovered that in fact Callas had never recorded the song. It was one of the myths that adhered to the singer after she died.

In return, Aki gave him what sounded like standard chirpy pop with an uplifting message, a sunny eighties ditty, 'Wonderful Life'. The singer called himself Black and had a pleasing melancholy baritone. Ullis played the song a couple of times and forgot about it. He liked the melody and he was always happy to be uplifted but for some reason the song didn't stay with him. It wasn't until they moved to Delhi that he heard it for what it was. Aki liked to play it in the morning as she was getting dressed for work. One morning the power failed at their Defence Colony apartment, and she sang the song all by herself as she tried and discarded this or that outfit. Her version of 'Wonderful Life' enhanced the vocal inflection and the sweetness of the melody, but it was when she got to the second verse and chorus that he heard the sadness that should have been apparent all along. It was then that he saw the scare quotes around the word 'wonderful'.

In the car as they were driving to her office, he asked why she was so taken with the song. He liked it too but only because he'd heard her sing it. For Aki it was different. She was dedicated to the song and had been for as long as he'd known her. Almost, he said, like it was some sort of obsession.

"I used to watch the video on MTV at my aunt's house," Aki said in a halting voice. "I used to put the television on hoping the video would play. I must have been five or six. There was a Golden Oldies programme that showed it all the time. I liked how clean-cut the singer was in his clean white shirt and short haircut. I liked the black-and-white images of happy people who weren't so happy really. I could see their smiles were strained at the edges. Colin's smile was different. It was real. The look on his face when he sang the line about needing a friend to make him happy. I couldn't believe how shy he was. Why was he performing if he was so shy? I liked it that in the video he never looked at the camera except once and then he looked terrified. There was something about him but I didn't know what it was. I thought about it and thought about it and one day it came to me. He'd been appearing in my dreams. That's why he seemed so familiar. He always said the same thing in the dream, that he needed a friend so he wouldn't be so alone. He had the same sweet smile as in the video. The main thing was his shyness. I felt sorry for him."

Driving in Delhi, most of his attention focused on the traffic, Ullis was struck by the tenderness in her voice. Her words came slowly, interspersed with long pauses, as if she was talking about an old friend from whom she had become estranged over some small slight that neither could remember.

"Many years later I looked for him on the internet, Colin? He wasn't fresh-faced any more but grizzled. The clean-cut handsome look was gone. His long hair was messy and frizzed out. Almost I didn't recognise him, though the sweetness was still there. You just had to look for it. Anyway, there was an interview where he said how messed up he was when he wrote the song. He'd been in a couple of car crashes and he was broke and the 'wonderful life' was all balls. Actually it was his way of being sarcastic. It wasn't wonderful at all, life. And then I thought, wait a minute, a *couple* of crashes? How do you get into a *couple* of crashes?"

Driving in Delhi, Ullis knew how easy it was to get into a couple of crashes. All he had to do was let his mind drift for a second or two. All he had to do was to sink into the tone of her voice as she spoke about the singer, her voice that was sadness beyond consolation. If he let himself think about it they would surely crash.

"He said in the interview that he had tried to write other songs over the years but every time he tried he realised it wouldn't be good enough. It wouldn't be anywhere as good as his big hit, 'Wonderful Life'. He'd try to write and he'd give up in frustration. I thought, how self-destructive must he be to compare everything to the best thing? No wonder he calls himself Black. No wonder he will never be happy. I asked myself the same question you asked. Why was I so taken by this song and this singer? Did it mean I was depressed? Do you think so?"

"I don't know," Ullis said. The truth was he did think so. But saying it would only depress her further.

"And that was when I wondered if he was still around. What was he up to? Was he on an endless 'Wonderful Life' tour? An old man with a beat-up guitar, and wherever he went all they wanted to hear was the song he wrote when he was a beautiful youth. That was all his life amounted to. One beautiful song,"

Aki said very softly, her voice so anguished he could hardly bear it. "He wasn't on a tour, Dommie. Can you guess how he died? It's all so obvious."

Driving in Delhi, not really listening, Ullis responded in a distracted manner he would later regret. "I couldn't possibly," he said, as they turned into the high-rise in which Aki's office was located. "I couldn't, guess I mean." By then he'd parked and she was hurriedly gathering her things because she was always a little late. She didn't get a chance to tell him how Colin had died and he forgot to mention it that evening or on the evenings that followed. It was one of the things he put off for later. After all, they were married. They were husband and wife. There would always be time for the small things.

Now as the nameless soprano betrays a slight inflection of anguish, Ullis goes to Black's Wikipedia page and scrolls to 'Death' and knows what he will find before he finds it. Cause of death: car crash. But what kind of crash? Who was driving? The page doesn't say. Ullis shakes a small hillock of meow meow to the back of his phone. He chops with a fingernail and snorts with a ten-rupee note. The powder leaves a vile satisfactory burn. Throwing back his head to allow the meow free passage into his synapses, he gets another close-up view of the purple-and-gold python-skin ceiling of the cab. It causes water to spring from his eyes. He winds down the window and a salt breeze explodes into the car. He takes a photo of the sea foregrounded by the angular black-and-yellow stripes of the kerb. Out of a dull white haze the city's faded skyline comes into view. Pylons loom like sails on a giant M. Near the rocky shore he sees the white bird whose name rhymes with regret. Ullis thinks he'd be happy to do this all day, to sit in a cab and listen to 'Ave Maria' on loop as the Sea Link soars above him and its cables match the soprano strut for strut.

From the Worli end of the bridge another view of the white ship, fixed in time, white against the white dazzle from the water.

The cab hit city traffic when they left the bridge. Slowly they inched past Sophia College, which Aki had briefly attended when her parents were still together, trundled past Chowpatty and Wilson College, where he had enrolled for a year when he first arrived in Bombay, sped past Charni Road and Marine Lines, a walk he and Aki had taken when he wanted to show her his version of the city, slowed past Sea Green Hotel, where they had once spent a rainy night, much of it naked on a balcony facing the Arabian Sea, and swerved past the coffee shop on the corner where they met a waiter who was the exact image of the exiled writer Manto, down to the owlish glasses and air of bleary civility.

At Churchgate Station he told the driver to wait and went into the wine shop at Asiatic, the city's first 'departmental' store when it opened in the mid-seventies. In the era of planned socialism the store appeared out of nowhere, a great gleaming portal of consumerist glory. Ullis and his friends would pennilessly walk around its air-conditioned interiors purely for the thrill of it. Asiatic's days of glamour were long gone. The shelves were dusty and mostly bare, and the shop had the look of a relic from the Soviet era. The alcohol was stocked at the front, on a single shelf behind a cash register. He asked for a bottle of Grey Goose or Cîroc. Neither was in stock and he had to settle for a dusty bottle of Jim Beam. The bored man at the counter tore himself away from his phone long enough to throw in a free backpack as part of a Jim Beam promotion.

In the cab, he dusted the bottle and cracked it open and took a rejuvenating sip. To meow or not to meow? It wasn't much of a question. He opened the baggie and noted with alarm that the contents had depleted inexplicably. There was only a negligible bit of powder left, most of which he felt compelled to snort immediately. Strangely the drug's effects seemed to have deteriorated in a matter of hours. It provided only two of the three qualities a discerning user should expect. A sense of speed and nausea, yes, but where was the numbness? Where was the paranoia? And where oh where was the much-touted crash? "Where are the feasts we were promised?" he said aloud, evincing an enthusiastic nod from the cabbie. The meow was unpleasant and unsatisfactory in every way. It had been designed to tranquillise animals, not stimulate humans. Ridiculous that people actually paid for this nonsense, thought Ullis, as he prepared another hit. He noted that the driver was a good man, an exemplary fellow who politely looked away while Ullis carried out his noisy business.

At the Taj, he paid the cabbie and tipped him and placed the box of ashes and bottle of Jim into his new backpack. He had to put the backpack through security. Strangely, they didn't ask to examine the contents of the box. They didn't pat him down or check his pockets when he beeped past the metal detector. A lapse. Lightning sometimes struck twice at the same place. He could have had a machine pistol strapped to his thigh or grenades in his underwear. With the backpack secured, he tripped a little as he fell up the stairs and into the lobby.

Inside, the crowd was thick: a cross-section of the unruly. He took some photos of punters walking aimlessly on the ridged carpets as they gawked at the ceiling and the floor and each other. Then, exhausted, he sank into a couch near an arrangement of low black-marble tables and caught a glimpse of his reflection in a mirror and looked quickly away, preferring not to dwell on the bruised eyes and frightening pallor.

Near him a child of four or five pulled against his mother's tight grip. When she turned to pick up her handbag, the boy slipped free and ran full tilt for the exit. She sprinted after him. Just five paces from freedom he was caught and brought back to the couch. He fell dramatically to the carpet, clutching his head as if he'd been shot.

"Mama," he said, "blood will come."

"Blood will not come," said his mother calmly. "Stop it, Himanshu."

"Yeah, Himanshu," said Ullis, getting up. "Take a Valium."

At the top of his voice Himanshu sang, "Valley-yum, valley-yum!" When he saw Ullis disappearing around the corner, he waved and improvised, "Tata bye-bye valley-yum."

At the coffee shop, Ullis was shown to a table by the long windows that faced the Gateway of India. Out there was the sea. Today it was calm. Today it was a picturesque surface for gently undulating commuter boats. He was far enough away not to see the garbage that swarmed against the sea wall at high tide. This alone, it seemed to him, made the coffee shop's overpriced bill of fare pay for itself many times over. Somebody asked what he would like. He ordered a croissant and a double macchiato. Thin metal screens with cut-outs in a kind of camouflage pattern covered one wall. He watched as a young man in white painstakingly sprayed and wiped each cut-out. His coffee arrived quickly with a brown bear imprinted on the foam.

"Would you like some sugar with your macchiato, sir?" said the waitress.

"No thanks," he replied. "I'm not in the habit of putting contaminants in my beverage."

The waitress's smile was full of pity.

"Of course not, sir," she said soothingly, as if she were speaking to an overactive child, to Himanshu for instance.

He waited until the annoyingly perceptive waitress had left and then he downed most of the bear in a single gulp. The man in white had finished cleaning each cut-out on the screen and was ensuring there was no dirt on the immaculate floors. Ullis finished the coffee and wondered what to do with his hands. He tried to tune out the piped-in sitar music but it was both subtle and insistent. Perhaps a Ravi Shankar sample updated for the wellness age? It was like flying Air India in the days when there was no other choice of airline: you were always oppressed by Ravi's sitar as you tried to find your seat.

At a table nearby, a man in a tracksuit rolled an unlit cigar between his fingers. He was speaking to a woman in a sari, who looked familiar in a possibly generic way. She wore silver hair and silver jewellery and a silvery smile. It was early in the day but there was a snifter of cognac in front of the man, an oily impresario type whose long hair was dyed red with henna. Ullis, who was nothing if not impressionable, waved for the waitress and ordered a cognac too. She raised an eyebrow and produced her maddening smile and went away. He smeared the croissant with strawberry jam and took a bite. It was his first or second taste of food in twenty-four hours and it left him with a sudden and unmistakable craving for meow meow.

Carefully he retrieved the baggie and examined it under the table. The contents were no less meagre than the last time he had looked, admittedly only a few minutes earlier. He upended the bag on the back of his phone and balanced the phone on his thigh. He found the rolled up ten-rupee note in his jacket pocket. When he bent forward to snort the last of the powder the phone slipped off his leg and fell noisily to the floor. Nobody seemed to notice. On his knees he searched for fallen meow among croissant crumbs and pepper flakes and sundry bits of debris. He pressed an index finger to what might have been powder and snorted it noisily and noticed someone beside him, the silvery sari from the next table.

"Are you all right?" she said. "You don't *look* it. Do you need some help, darling? Whatever *are* you doing?"

Dominic Ullis stood up reluctantly, though not without dignity. "I'm fine," he said. "I seem to have dropped my phone."

"Do you remember me? We were on the same flight yesterday from Dilli. I was sitting next to you. But it's the most charming coincidence! Of all the people to bump into at breakfast! What are the chances? Wait, *don't* you remember?"

"Yes, of course I remember," he said politely.

"You don't," she said, delighted. "You don't remember at *all*. What's my name?"

There was a comfortable silence.

"Naughty boy," she said. "I'm Payal. Payal! And you're Ulysses, aren't you?"

"Ullis," he replied. "Indian, not Greek."

"Right, Ulysses. You're welcome to join us if you're sitting alone and everything?"

She manoeuvred him gently to her table, where the man with the hennaed hair had emptied the snifter and continued to examine his unlit cigar. The waitress returned with Ullis's cognac and a silver bowl of salted nuts. A gleaming young man in a suit and tie retrieved the Jim Beam backpack and placed it on a chair beside him.

"Oh dear," said Payal, gesturing at the man. "He's wearing a black suit rather similar to yours. If you don't want to be mistaken for a waiter, darling, do sit down and take off your coat."

"I don't mind being mistaken for a waiter," said Ullis. "It's an honest job. We owe them a lot more than tips. But I'll certainly take your suggestion into consideration."

"A joke," she said. "How dreadful. Now, it seems to me that if you gentlemen are drinking cognac first thing in the morning, well then I must too, mustn't I? I mean you've practically *twisted* my arm, ha ha. A mimosa, Jennifer, for me."

"Of course, Madam Payal," said Jennifer, whose manner had changed entirely, who didn't raise an eyebrow, who was positively simpering with pleasure.

Positioning himself in front of his snifter, Ullis sat down and nodded distractedly at the man with the interesting hair. Everything seemed properly arranged for once. He was a stranger at a stranger's table. He was a stranger to himself. This was correct. This was exactly as it should be.

"Forgive me," said Payal, taking a seat. "Ulysses, this is Feroze. Feroze, Ulysses."

A beaming waiter appeared at her elbow. He bore a flute filled to the brim with orange bubbles. She lifted it off the tray.

"To opportune meetings, darlings, on airplanes and off," said Payal, smiling terrifically.

"To sensible investments," said Feroze. "To helping our friends make the correct ones."

"To cognac in the morning," said Ullis, "and all the unsung waiters of the world."

They drank and Feroze resumed his argument, conducted in a peremptory yet wheedling voice that did little to help his case.

"You see," he said, "thanks to the internet, news is available to us as it occurs anywhere in the world at any time of day or night. My advice is always the same. Why invest in cricket or horse racing when you can invest in yourself? That is the way forward."

"Yaar," said Payal. "This is all so beastly boring. Let's go to the pool."

"Cannot," said Feroze. "Some have to work. I take it you will not be investing, not today at least?"

"Not today, darling," said Payal unhappily.

"Then I shall smoke my cigar and push off. Will you join me in the smoking area?"

"Why don't you boys go ahead? I'll be poolside finishing my mimosa and soaking up my ultraviolet."

They stepped through French doors into an open area with ashtrays on marble stands. Feroze offered a cigar. Around them was a high wall and white latticework that screened the street from the hotel's elegant guests. Or, thought Ullis, perhaps it was the other way around. Screen the guests and their lives of carelessness from the hoi polloi, postpone the revolution for a minute.

"Are you an old friend of Payal's?" said Feroze.

Ullis was suddenly cautious.

"Yes," he replied, wincing at the lie. "And you?"

"I consider myself a friend but I think she sees me as a business acquaintance."

"And what is your business?"

"I take bets," said Feroze, lighting both their cigars. "The wilder the better. Payal's bets as you probably know are very much wild, like tigers in Ranthambore."

44

"You mean you're a bookie?"

"That's a word we try to avoid, if you know what I mean?"

"Oh," said Ullis, conspiratorially puffing, "I most certainly do."

"As I was telling Payal, I've known her since she was a small child but that doesn't mean I will act like a yes man when I know she is making a bad decision."

"But isn't that what it means to be an adult? The freedom to make your own bad decisions?"

Feroze sucked at his cigar and regarded Ullis for a moment, wondering if he could be enlisted in persuading Payal. He thought not. And so they smoked in silence. From time to time Ullis blew on his cigar to make it burn evenly. He was trying to enjoy it: though slightly stale it was Cuban and properly expensive.

In the sun Feroze's long hair had turned scarlet. He tucked it behind his ears and retrieved a large phone from his briefcase. There was Urdu or Persian calligraphy tattooed on his forearm.

"So, business is calling and I must answer," he said. He ground his cigar into an ashtray and nodded to himself.

From where Ullis stood, the Gateway of India across the street was just visible through the latticework. Not that there was much to see since the monument had become a mess of police barricades. Built to welcome King George V to his Indian holdings, the Gateway hadn't aged well. It was grimy and uncared for and permanently shut. After the terrorist attack that had partially destroyed the hotel in 2008, visitors were no longer welcome to the old monument across the street. But there was a time when it had been available for any kind of unsavoury activity. Ullis and his associates had used its high-ceilinged darkness to shoot up heroin, a difficult feat because the smell of urine was so overpowering it caused even hardened junkies to gag.

What had become of the junkies and flower children of Bombay? Where was Srinivas Acharya, better known as Archie, who liked to raise his syringe in a toast "to good King George"? "Praise the nod," he'd intone and make a priestly sign of the cross before plugging his ears with his fingers, the better to experience the rush. Where had they gone, those eaters and shooters and sniffers of pleasure? Dead, of course: infinitely dead. His friends and enemies dead, his wife dead, everybody dead, except for me and my monkey.

Not everybody. One at least of the old junkies was alive. The year before, Ullis had made a quick trip to Bombay to read at a poetry event with Anne Waldman. They'd driven into the city in the same car. The Beat writer and poet had wanted to buy some Indian music. Because they were early he suggested they stop at Rhythm House for CDs. The music store had been a favourite venue during his college years. He and his friends would cut class to smoke chillums and sample vinyl at the free listening cubicles for hours, or until they were asked politely to leave by the sympathetic staff. Ullis and Waldman had spent most of the ride into Colaba talking about Waldman's friend, the junkie poet Jim Carroll, whose early work Ullis had admired. According to Waldman, Carroll too had been a labourer in the vineyard of the virus. Ullis was alarmed to learn that Carroll had been killed by the same alphabetic strain of hepatitis that he carried. It had brought the New York poet closer to home than was strictly comfortable. After the sobering ride they went into Rhythm House where, prowling the aisles like a ghost from the past, was Hormazd, his old friend, who told Ullis in detail about his own tryst with hepatitis C and his experience with interferon and the fact that the virus was always present, cunning and dormant, waiting for the right moment to strike. In the presence of the ghostly Hormazd and the ghost of Jim Carroll, Ullis had felt the pull of both the past and the future. To deal with the double set of aggravations, he had gone alone to a bar near the Regal Cinema and ordered several double whiskies with a beer back. Of course he'd missed the reading.

Haloed by cigar smoke, Ullis took out his phone and scrolled through the contact list for Danny Blow.

"Danny?"

"Yus?"

"Dom here."

"Sir, long time no see."

"I was thinking the exact same thing."

"Are you in Bombay, sir?"

"In Colaba. I'm wondering if we could meet."

"Sure, bro," said Danny. "Will take me some time, yus?"

They set a time and Ullis ended the call.

When he had had enough Cuban smoke, he let the cigar smoulder in an ashtray and went back to the table where his cognac stood unmolested. He resolved to pick up a little something if only for auld lang syne: a twist of coke, perhaps stabilised by a pudi of Bombay brown. The combination would leave him perfectly poised between the high and the low. He was rubbing his hands in anticipation when Jennifer appeared.

"Is there anything I can help you with, sir?"

"I was weighing the pros and cons of certain substances, a comparative study," he said brightly, because it was important to maintain the appearance of brightness. "I think the pros are winning."

Jennifer smiled politely, who most likely knew of no substances stronger than tea or coffee, whose only truck with a virus was the flu, whose rose-milk complexion conveyed the freshness only a good night's sleep could provide.

"Madam asked me to show you to the pool," she said. "Please follow me."

He carried his cognac through a corridor to the lobby of the old wing and out through glass doors into the sun. Stepping into the glitter off the pool, he grabbed one-handedly in his jacket for sunglasses.

The sight of the blue water brought a small rush of memory. In all the years he had lived in the neighbourhood in his twenties, walking past the hotel at all times of day and night, it had never struck him that the building faced the wrong way, until one morning he'd been going up Mandlik Road towards the sea, the tiny road directly facing the Taj, and he saw the front facade lit up by the sun, saw it as if for the first time, and knew that the old rumour had been true all along.

The pool had been constructed in what had originally been the hotel's front entrance, where horse carriages took guests past the wrought-iron gates and along the great courtyard. The back of the hotel served as the front. It was a plainer, less imposing facade and it had welcomed oblivious visitors for more than a hundred years. To disguise the error, the front had been barred long ago and the gates permanently shut, the pool dug in the middle of the front lawns and palm trees planted to hide the great gates and the driveway. As a result the pool was set off by the hotel's true face, a soaring centre dome with twin wings. The guests sunning themselves by the water had no idea about the building's history, that a gigantic mistake had been made, followed by a creative decades-long effort to cover it up: one of the great hotels of the world, built the wrong way round, facing the city rather than the sea. It wasn't until you stood at the far end of the pool or on Mandlik Road that you saw it the way it would have been if only the hotel had owned its mistake and opened up the gates and proudly faced the wrong way.

Payal was lying on a blue and white striped towel, her upper body in the shade of a tilted umbrella. She wore a one-piece turquoise swimsuit and had not removed her heavy jewellery or watch. Her hair was perfectly dry, not to mention coiffed. It didn't look as if she had any intention of entering the freshly chlorinated water. Jennifer said "Madam," bowed and left.

Ullis considered doffing his jacket but the meow meow and cognac enveloped him in a climate-controlled bubble into which no heat would penetrate. He stretched out fully dressed with a view of the central dome. He crossed his loafer-clad feet and let the fumes of the cognac clear his muddied head. But an air hammer started up somewhere on the Causeway. He heard a motorcycle and the high cry of a black kite. The light on the water was liturgical, blinding, Saul-light on the road to conversion.

"Enough sun for me," said Payal. She sat up. "I'm ready for lunch, if you really want to know. Come along, won't you?"

"All right."

"You're not a rapist or thief, are you?"

"Not to the best of my knowledge, no. And this is a bit rich coming from someone who steals airline cutlery."

"But I *always* steal the cutlery on flights, darling, it comes in handy when you're fighting off creditors," she said. "Did Feroze leave or is he still here, overstaying his welcome as usual?"

"I believe he took off."

"Good, good. He's always asking for money and sticking me with the bill for his booze. He thinks I'm flush because I have a permanent room at the hotel. He has no idea I don't have a sou."

"Have you tried telling him? Sometimes the direct approach works wonders. Feroze is a bookie. His job is to bet on you losing. The more you bet, the less likely you are to win. If he knew you had no ready cash he might back off some. It's certainly worth a try."

Payal considered him speculatively. She said, "I think that's the longest string of words I've heard you utter since we met, darling."

They'd only just met but she was absolutely correct. It was the most he had said in days, if not weeks, and it had tired him out. Lunar tiredness, more ebb than flow. Like the pool's shaky blue lines.

"You're right, you're right," Payal continued. "I'm so tired of betting on slow horses and slower batsmen. For goodness' sake, I'm a *girl*. I want to have fun, what's wrong with that?" She put a robe over her swimsuit and picked up her phone. "Listen, I'm having friends over this evening at my place in Alibag. It's a bit of a trek, I know, but you're welcome to come."

"Sure," said Ullis, repeating the phrase that was becoming his motif: "I don't see why not."

"Lovely, but first could you settle the bill? I'm not allowed to order alcohol, darling, it's the bane of my life. Next stop, my room. I'll organise everything else, I promise."

Two hotel employees followed them upstairs. One carried Payal's toiletries and sunglasses. The other held the lift open and showed her the way to her quarters. In case she'd forgotten where she lived.

"I wonder if you could do me a huge favour," said Payal, once they were ensconced in her suite with the panoramic view of the

Arabian Sea. The picture window framed distant ships and cold eternal whitecaps. "Could you go out and get us something to drink, something in the realm of vodka possibly? I can order *anything* on room service except the fun stuff. I've been banned by the fam."

"Payal, you're in luck," said Ullis. He brought out the almost new bottle of Jim from his backpack (checking first that the white box was still there, resting undisturbed). "It isn't in the realm of vodka but it is most definitely in the realm of alcohol."

Payal actually clapped her hands and said, "Yay?"

He found glasses and ice and poured the bourbon and downed his drink and poured another, which he attempted sedately to sip. His legs felt wobbly for some reason. There was a pressing need for reinforcements, a booster shot, a maintenance dose, a renewed layer of protection (something, anything to postpone the inevitable crash, and the regret): he was in a hurry to meet Danny Blow.

"And now if you'll excuse me I'm going to step outside for a minute. I have some chores to take care of."

"Take my number," said Payal.

CHAPTER FOUR

Blurred by the cognac and Jim, empty stomach pleasantly burning, he descended the wide carpeted staircase of the palace wing and made a second call.

"Ten minutes, sir," said Danny.

"When you call me sir," Ullis said, "I feel like I should get a haircut."

"Yus, sir."

"And brush up on my PowerPoint skills."

"Yus," Danny said, sounding distracted, "meet me across from the Asiatic. Okay, bro?"

"Okay, bro."

Framed by the great floating staircase, the hotel's central dome was a kaleidoscope of backlit sea green, or Wedgwood blue possibly, with a touch of white at the centre. From below it was interesting without being striking. Who would guess at the grandeur of the exterior, the red dome visible from miles away, so proud a symbol of the city that it had become a target for terrorism from across the border? But this was not the time to gawk. Dominic Ullis was a man with a renewed sense of mission. He hurried out of the hotel and waved down a taxi.

He'd met Danny in the early 2000s when cocaine descended on the city like a dirty white blanket. One night at a gallery opening in Lower Parel, Ullis sampled a line of product so clean he had to enquire as to its provenance. He'd been directed to the DJ. On the decks he found a guy in a beanie rapping over basic drum and bass. The raps were popular with the crowd but impossible to decipher. A sign of the times, thought Ullis, incomprehensibility as reward. They got to know each other over the course of a mild Bombay winter. Danny didn't consider himself a dealer. He said he was a musician who liked to help out his friends in return for a small commission. He was always available and always cheerful. He seemed never to sleep. He preferred text messages to phone calls. Soon Ullis came to think of Danny's texts as a new form of communication with a distant, baffling connection to English.

On cue his phone buzzed with a message.

"Hello Sir, 25m. U need 1 or 2? Lil discount on 2!"

As usual the message was much too explicit. It was entirely possible that Danny's phone had fallen into the hands of the police in whose clutches the dealer languished while they set traps for his clients. It had happened once before. The cops had made a note of every number on Danny's phone and let him go. Ever since, Ullis had wondered if his calls were tapped, his texts checked, his photos leered at, graded and filed. In the sudden clasp of druggy paranoia he yearned for the glass of Jim he had left on Payal's coffee table. In his professional opinion Danny wasn't careful enough while texting, and he texted all day long. He didn't bother with code. He addressed his buyers by name. He carried product in a psychedelic fanny pack. They usually met on deserted streets, each arriving in a separate car. Out Danny would step, a Nigerian in Bombay, sporting a beanie in the muggy midnight heat. He'd saunter over and lean in and exchange a plastic bag for cash. As if he wanted to tempt the gods to do their worst. As if he did not know that the gods, even at their best, were not to be trifled with.

It was early in the day. The sun shone and shone, beating on Ullis's head like a gong. For relief he moved into the shade of a locksmith's shop, the green awning and concrete porch a small oasis of coolness. Above him in the plane trees a tailorbird cried, "Cut, cut, cut."

A creature of habit, he sent Aki a text: "Waiting 4 the man, I thought U should know!" If he scrolled up he would find her last messages, sent on the night of her death. He had read them in the daze of amnesia and he'd retained nothing. He needed to read them again, but he couldn't do it. He didn't have the time. Also, as his mother (and John Berryman's) would say, he had no inner resources. He was all out of resources, inner and outer. He needed distraction and fortification. Scrolling single-mindedly, he found a video of the American president speaking at a podium in front of a bank of Stars 'n' Stripes. The sky was very blue and the presidential face very orange, except for two startlingly pasty oval spots around the eyes.

"America," he said, then paused for the cameras and raised his index finger, "first."

"You mean Russia first," said Ullis, nodding gleefully.

The president's words filled his head with ballast, like gravel in the bilge to stop a ship from capsizing. The president filled his head with gravel and it served as a welcome and necessary substitute for thought. The president's words, the white power signals he made to the cameras, his physical bulk, all of it kept Ullis from capsizing. Already, thanks to the president's considerable theatrical gifts, Ullis's bruised mind had stopped alighting as frequently and obsessively on the set of images built around his wife's face swinging at an angle above him. The president, a master of distraction, had this effect. This was why he needed plenty of screen time with the man, first thing in the morning and last thing at night, if possible. It was the only thing that helped him sleep, hearing that unmistakable voice, the crazed floating lullaby. The president would move his hands as if he were playing an invisible accordion and Ullis would hear music. The president would say something demonstrably untrue while making a comical expression and Ullis would smile tremulously, with undisguised gratitude. The president's comb-over was a scientific impossibility and his gestures grandiose. His instinct was to be vile and petty and naysaying. Yet his self-assurance grew from scandal to scandal. It was edifying, a spectacle from the fall of the Roman Empire. Ullis relied upon the expertise with which the president had turned the daily news into a genre of reality television. He was devoted to the image of the man, to his bitter humour and sense of endless grievance. The way he pronounced 'Puerto Rico' by humorously rolling his 'r's while the afflicted were allowed to perish. The way he took everything personally, from climate change to the stock market. What would happen if he were to leave the stage? What would Ullis do with his time? Like the rest of the world, he would be bereft. He would have to go into rehab. A realisation struck him with the force of prophecy: the American president's wellbeing affected his own. He hoped the man was there to stay, in or out of office.

Another buzz. A message, as prime a piece of Dannyana as any he had received: "Got me this time excellent stone white stuff on rock form untouch plus cooked one crack n lsd crystal mdma n h-in. If you need any good one let me know. Tkcr Brother. C u latr."

Did Danny really think it was okay to list crack, LSD, crystal meth and MDMA in a text, but heroin alone required a coy 'h-in'? What was wrong with him? Perhaps he *had* been caught by a wily policeman and all this was an elaborate ruse. To distract himself, Ullis tried out Danny's text in rap cadence: *Crack 'n' LSD 'n' crystalline / mdma 'n' h-dash-in.* It didn't work. Something was missing, something with the heft of classic rap. He tried again, this time adding gang hand signage (faux, of course) and immediately it began to sound better.

Pity poor Ullis anxiously waiting across the street from the Asiatic Library, making devil horns and white power signals while passersby gave him a wide and frightened berth. Pity him obediently waiting in the doorway of a locksmith's shop like a large furless creature unaccustomed to daylight. He'd been late getting there and had wondered for a brief wild moment if Danny would be waiting. Of course he was not. Rule number one in the dealer's handbook: never be on time. Not even Danny the Rapper would consider breaking this commandment. Then, just as if Danny had read his mind or heard it on the junkie jungle telegraph, there was the buzz of a text: "10m bro".

Above him in the trees the tailorbird scolded in real time, "Cut!"

Perhaps it was a sign from the world around him. Perhaps the bird was telling him to cut and run while the cutting was good. How many times had he waited for dealers in the crummiest corners of this or that city? If he could collect the time he had spent, what would it amount to? (Not much.) And what would he do with the time saved? (Waste it, of course.) And since he was in the mood for questions: What was the lure of the high? Now there was a question a sensible person would duck, simply because the answer was so plain, so ruinous. You paid in money and time for a drug that obliterated money and time. You received the peace of eternal rest. Your breath slowed to glacial increments. Your fears flatlined. You dreamed with your eyes open and you conversed with those you loved. You died your best death and you came back to life. Or you didn't. It was the greatest of all lures. It was beauty. It was hope.

Twenty minutes later, a black SUV stopped to honks of protest from other cars. A small man under a giant Afro peered from the back seat.

"Sir," Danny said, beckoning.

Ullis got into the car and the driver eased back inside the traffic.

"You are not looking so good, sir," said Danny, who was not looking so good either. His skin had mottled into splotches of dusty cream and his eyes were red and glazed. "You don't believe in sleeping, no?"

"No," said Ullis. "Nice to see you too, Danny."

"Man, why you wearing a suit?"

"I had to go to a formal occasion," said Ullis as they bumped fists. "Nothing wrong with a bit of formality."

"Bro, damn good crack," said Danny mysteriously.

"Shall we get to the business at hand?" Ullis pulled out a wad of five hundred-rupee notes. To his surprise Danny waved it away.

"Keep for now. We going to my friend's house," said Danny, patting the iridescent pouch he wore across his belly. The pouch sported a trippy day-glo Grateful Dead design, of all things. Hopeless, subterfuge was hopeless. Danny might as well wear a placard that said, DRUG DEALER!

"Do me a favour, bro," the dealer said. He offered Ullis a pair of earphones. "Check my new track." This was a ritual when buying drugs from Danny. He touched play on his phone, and Ullis heard a spare beat and three-note piano line overlaid by tinny bass. Danny's voice dialled in, cracked and grizzled, railing against

God, hoes, racists and the dilution of the black bloodline. There was a percussion solo and a coda praising "Malcolm X / The man who hex / Goin' off like SFX," and there the track ended, just as Ullis was beginning to enjoy it.

"What you think? Deadly or what?" said Danny, grinning widely. "Go on, bro."

"Deadly! Just, I think you shouldn't have stinted on the 'hoes' and 'motherfuckers'. I only counted about twenty. It's hip-hop, too much is never enough."

"You got a point though," said Danny, as the car turned under a bridge. They stopped on a short covered street lined on both sides with parked lorries and handcarts. Danny gave the driver money. He said, "Man, wait right here!"

The road under the bridge was cobbled and terrifically uneven. Ullis noticed a bundle of black feathers, a dead crow collapsed into itself, as if its internal organs had been sucked out leaving only a vacuum of beak and eyes, and feathers glossy in the sodium light. Nearby a striped cat crouched, weighing its options.

They walked towards Opera House and passed a huddle of street vendors. There was a roadside 'shoe repair expert' and a locksmith. There was a cart selling Bombay sandwiches. Ullis watched as white Wibs bread was spread with green chutney and Amul butter and layered with paper-thin slices of tomato and onion and boiled potato. He felt a sudden flare of hunger, crushed immediately by the mutant meow-fed butterflies in his belly. They walked on.

The sun, brighter and hotter than ever, beat against air heavy with gas and laden with chemicals. *Twelve more years.* They turned into a gated house, and a uniformed guard led them to a small steel-lined claustrophobia-inducing elevator. To distract himself on the way down he recalled Aki's exact words: *Twelve more years and life as we know it is over.* It had taken much less than twelve years for their life to be over. Looking around, he made the mistake of catching sight of himself in the mirror. Danny was right. He wasn't looking so good. The sight of the emaciated strange-eyed man – dark shadows pockmarked by white stubble – made him want to exit the elevator, the day, his life, go somewhere far from mirrors and the rising sea, where he would relearn the lost and tender art of sleeping, where he would hear again his wife's loving tirade break like the ocean around his head. Then, instead of Lowell, he heard Franz Wright's whispery voice dripping into his ear a choice piece of cracked advice: *the avoidance of mirrors represents one of humankind's major ordeals among the stars . . .* Ullis gazed obediently at his loafers until at last the steel doors opened at the basement. He exited gratefully and stopped short at the sight of a uniformed policeman. Danny-wards he looked for guidance.

"Hey, Damodar," said Danny to the cop. "What up?"

"Danny," said Damodar, whose blue cap was set at a jaunty angle. He knocked on a panelled door and it opened at once as if someone had been standing there waiting to be signalled.

"Welcome to the bunker," said a tall man with watery eyes and salt-and-pepper hair. His heavy belly began at the breastbone. He pulled Ullis into the room with a sweaty handshake that left a red pressure mark on the back of his hand.

"This is Anis, our host," said Danny. "Dom is a writer."

"Oh yes?" said his host. "Which movie? Maybe I saw it."

"Not that kind of writer," said Ullis. "Unfortunately."

"Dom is a poet and he know it," said Danny, "sometimes he show it and sometimes he grow it."

"Woah," said Ullis hastily, "not true. I'm no poet."

"Yes, sir, you are," said Danny.

"You're a poet only when you're writing," said Ullis.

Anis clapped his hands. "Poetries? Very nice, very nice, I also like. Rupee Crore is my favourite!"

"You mean Rupi Kaur?"

"Yes, yes. My girl Rupee writes milk and honey, bastard!" He produced a laugh like broken glass, thick with phlegm and pleasure.

"When you're not writing, you're just another chooth," said Ullis. "I haven't written anything in a long time."

"Come with me, chooth," said Anis, putting a meaty paw on his shoulder and steering him to the bar.

A dinner party at noon, the air thick with eau de cologne and cigarette smoke. Heavy gold curtains pulled against the light. Crochet doilies wilted on the fake French furniture. The walls crowded with tribal masks and paintings of jazz musicians. Candles flickered. There was music but it sounded indistinct, like noises from the bottom of the sea. The music and the voices and the dim undersea light, the smell of sweat and perfume and cleaning fluid: a vision out of the near future. A drowned nation, a league of drowned nations, a planet spawned by the devil and spurned by God, doom our only recourse.

But what right had Ullis to speak of God and the devil? What right had he to point fingers? Better to keep such ideas within the confines of one's head right up until the moment that the sea was lapping at one's knees. Say in about twelve years.

Reluctantly, he joined a group of men in gym clothes drinking brandy at the bar. In the electric gloom of the basement, their sweaty excited faces were wreathed in scarves of blue and yellow smoke. They spoke a monkey jabber of yelps and curses. The only woman in the room sat at a high table in the corner, arguing with a man in cargo shorts. Smoky yellow soot covered everything.

"Come here, bastard," Anis told a youth with a wispy goatee and a bombardier's stare. He put meaty hands on either side of the boy's face and kissed him on the lips. He crushed him in a bear hug. "Bastard!" he kept saying. "Ya bastard!"

Ullis looked for Danny who had cleverly vanished. He took out his phone and couldn't remember why. Someone appeared with a tray. There were glasses of red wine and cigarettes in a saucer. He took a cigarette and put it back when he remembered that he'd quit smoking. He called Danny and heard a recorded voice speaking in an accent that strove to be British: "This number does not exist."

He was in Hades. He was in Gehenna where numbers did not exist and humans became their demon counterparts. He was in hell and Danny was Virgil but Virgil was nowhere to be found. It was all of a piece, a fated trajectory he could not undo: his wife's death in Delhi, the electric flames of the crematorium, the descent into Bombay, the expense of the spirit, the inevitable waste of shame. He might as well give in and submit with good grace. Make himself at home in hell's smoky apartments.

There was the sudden sound of gunshots, Anis clapping his hands. "Victor," he said. "Drink, bring!" Had he won a wager, an argument, a feud? Whatever the nature of the win, the drink was not brought. Anis stood swaying on his feet. Ullis imagined him toppling over like a tree in a storm. He imagined the crash would reverberate through the house, from the basement to the top floors. Anis focused on a man standing alone near the air conditioner, smoking. A pair of tortoiseshell reading glasses hung on a chain around his neck.

"Dinshaw," said Anis. "Bastard, come here!"

He put his hand over Dinshaw's mouth and kissed him very hard. Dinshaw's cigarette fell to the floor, a burst of tiny sparks.

"Dinshaw, ya bastard," said Anis, holding him in a one-handed bear hug. "Tell everybody, didn't I give you two crores?"

"It was more than that," said Dinshaw, struggling to free himself. "But it wasn't enough. You still owe us."

Anis pulled him to the couch and kissed him again, his hand between their mouths. The struggle continued, until all of a sudden Anis got up and went to the woman at the corner table.

"I was a partner at Izzy," said Dinshaw when he saw that Anis had gone. He sounded exhausted.

"I remember Izzy," said Ullis. He recalled a Berlin dive in the heart of a district of disused textile mills. He recalled the floor at the entrance to the club, a smiley face made of coloured tiles. "I think everybody remembers Izzy. It shut too soon."

"Anis bought it from me and my partners. He stiffed us on the deal and shut it down."

"That's business," said Anis, who had stealthily returned. "Just remember, bastard, legends fuck alone. They don't bro up, okay?" He hitched his pants and squinted. Swaying on his feet, he glared at his guests as if he wanted to fight them one bastard at a time. He was a big man yearning for battle. And a drink.

"Victor!" he yelled. "Where's Victor?"

At last there arrived a diminutive barefoot man in a frayed polo shirt and house shorts. He bore a glass of whisky on a tray. His feet were white with age and dust. Curly greying hair, a pointed face, a tiny gold cross on a leather thong.

Anis took the drink and said, "Victor, bring!"

Victor went into the kitchen where he put a dinner plate into the microwave. When it had warmed sufficiently, he adorned the centre with slender lines of cocaine. There were grooves on the side, on which he placed some short plastic straws. He brought the offering around. Ullis took a line and passed it on, and Victor asked what he would like to drink. He returned immediately with a large Grey Goose on ice. Ullis felt the back of his throat go numb from the cocaine and he took a sip of vodka to enhance the numbness.

If I keep drinking I will shed my thoughts like old skin. If I keep drinking I will be thoughtless and free. If I keep drinking I won't have to speak ever again. I will die too and everything will work out, one way or the other.

He raised his glass and heard raised voices.

"If you touch me again I will call police," said the woman in the corner. She was perched on a barstool. Her short dress and rubber slippers were a size too large for her, as if she had suddenly lost weight. She was speaking to a Delhi television pundit famed for his shock of white hair and his Maserati and the allegations that sprouted around him like toadstools in the shade of the #MeToo movement. Ullis remembered that his name was Shabash. Usually photographed in bespoke suits, tonight he was off-duty, wearing cargo shorts and an ABBA T-shirt. Another man leaned against the wall. A bottle of mineral water dangled loosely from his hand.

"I'll vouch for this fellow," said Dinshaw. "He's a well-known impresario from Delhi. There's really no need to call the police."

"Ce? Taci!" said the woman. "I know who he is. Question is who are you?"

"Dinshaw's my name."

"Forget! I don't care."

"And you are?"

"I don't care! He slapped me. Ce naiba faci?"

"You laughed at me," said Shabash, running a hand through his thick white coif. "I'm not a dolt, you know. I expect better behaviour from my friends."

The story emerged. Shabash and the woman had been deep in conversation when Anis, walking past, pulled down Shabash's shorts and gave the room a glimpse of skimpy black Speedos. The woman was quick to guffaw. Shabash put his shorts back in place, his face a mask. Not a man to take lightly an assault on his dignity, and too much of a coward to tackle the true culprit, Shabash turned to the woman who had laughed at his humiliation and slapped her.

"I am Romanian woman from Romania," she said, holding up her cell phone. "I am not joking. Touch me again and I will call cops."

The man who had been leaning against the wall straightened up and said, "I am DCP with Mumbai police, madam. How can I help?"

Victor came by just then with a fresh plate of tiny lines. The woman and the policeman took a taste each but Shabash pointedly declined. When the plate came to Ullis he took two hits, one for each nostril. The powder hardly burned. The rush was clean and pharmaceutically sound, which meant the cocaine was top of the line. It had not been cut with lactose or crushed vitamins or mephedrone or ketamine. In short, it was Danny at his best.

He was sitting on the couch with his fingers in his ears in honour of the long-deceased Srinivas Acharya when he felt something sharp under his hips: a pair of tortoiseshell glasses, the chain broken during Anis's frenzied bear hug. He looked around the room and found Dinshaw smoking at his spot near the air conditioner.

"Man's a dick," said Dinshaw, accepting the spectacles.

"I think that isn't much of an exaggeration," said Ullis.

"Boss, I know it for a fact. We were schoolmates at St Mary's. He was the worst bully on the playground and he always picked on the smallest kids."

"He hasn't changed much."

"I think he's got worse. And it's the booze, not the coke. For some people alcohol is poison, yes? Like mainlining fucking arsenic."

"You're probably right, though I hate to speak badly of alcohol. I don't know where I'd be without it."

"Want to hear something? I was having a little chat with Mara, the Romanian? Victor pulled me away, physically pulled me away and told me Anis wouldn't like it. Like he owns her. Like he went to the market and bought her from her parents or something."

"What are you bastards talking?" said Anis. Smoke issued from his nostrils in twin streams, a bull with a nicotine habit.

"Actually we were talking about you," said Ullis.

"Oh yes? What were you talking about me?"

"We were wishing you weren't such a bully."

Dinshaw's cigarette froze in mid-air. Anis rotated his head from side to side like a boxer warming up for twelve rounds in the ring. He said, "Who are you anyway, man? You're a poet, not scriptwriter! Means, like, you're, like, nothing . . . like, nobody."

"You're right about that," said Ullis.

"Of course I am right," said Anis. "If you disappeared tomorrow who would notice?"

Ullis knew the truth when he heard it. There was little question that nobody would notice his disappearance, not from Bombay, not from Delhi, not from anywhere. The only person who might have noticed had been reduced to ashes in a box. He was alone in the world. Not that this was necessarily a bad thing. There was an advantage to being alone and anonymous: you *were* free to disappear if you wished. For some people vanishing off the face of the earth was an attractive proposition. He was about to explain this to his lumbering host when Anis picked up a bottle of whisky – Solan No. 1, of all the old-school drinks in the world – put it to his mouth and drank deeply. Was he preparing for battle? Why bother? Ullis felt as if he had been ground into the dust of the field and pulverised, never to rise again. He had been properly vanquished by Anis the Victor.

"Writer-ji," Anis began. His veiny right hand bunched into a fist.

Above Ullis's head a candelabrum of cigarette smoke descended by degrees. The lower it fell the more Ullis knew the truth of Anis's words, that he had indeed disappeared without anybody noticing. He steeled himself for the Anissian punch. Truth to tell, he looked forward to it. A well-aimed blow might be the very thing to clear away the cobwebs of confusion and guilt and misunderstanding. A broken nose or split lip would focus his mind and steady its course. He waited but the blow did not land. Instead, a well-tended Afro bobbed into view. Like an angel of reconciliation, Danny positioned himself between the two men. Ullis imagined he saw the white afterglow of giant wings. Danny's eyes, liquid and all-knowing, were the only source of tenderness in the room, perhaps in the entire city.

Oh angel, lead me out of the underworld, for I am sorely vexed and my spirit is low.

"Come with me," said Danny, as if in response to Ullis's unspoken prayer. He led the way into an adjoining room where a Hindi movie was projected on a wall-sized screen. A Bombay starlet executed a series of complicated twirls and lunges. Purple

67

sateen skirt. Puffy yellow sleeves. Snow White cosplay dress, face caked and emotionless, surrounded by a bevy of white back-up dancers. Where were they from? Tallinn? Zagreb? Bucharest? Birmingham? As in the French poet's decree: anywhere but here. How many centuries of patient indoctrination went into such a scene? Colonial India was alive and well in the movies at least. It was a comforting thought for a post-colonial from the post-colonies. He watched the screen, his eyes wide. The movie was on silent but there were subtitles and frequent ads. A series of montages of white people in Indian settings: an elderly lady attempting yoga, a couple in a luxury hotel, a young traveller biking on a mountain road. Each scene was followed by a logo: Incredible India! It was all so incredible that Ullis felt properly enslaved. Danny had to lead him by the arm to a spot in the middle of the room, away from the screen. There were chairs with half-tables attached to the armrests, for drinks to be placed and lines made. On a sideboard was a photo of a pleasantly smiling middle-aged woman and two small children.

"Anis's wife," said Danny, "and kids. She wants slow Indian divorce. House, kids, monies, she wants it all. He says he doesn't care except for the money."

When he ran out of gossip, Danny retrieved a plastic bubble from his pouch and held it under the track lights.

"Two grams is only ten thou with discount," said Danny.

"That's a little on the high side, Daniel," said Ullis.

"Sir, is not high, but you *will* get high like a spaceman. Pure rock. You try the material, you know. Best quality, bro. Pure, no cuts, no buts."

"What else do you have?" said Ullis, eagerly handing over five two thousand-rupee notes.

Danny unhooked his famous pouch and spread it open. From a flat pocket on the side he extracted business cards and gave one to Ullis. *Danny Blow*, it read, *Rapper, Producer, Entrepreneur*. There was a phone number and an email address and a *Daredevil* logo.

"Got some meow, some acid and this," Danny paused, pointing triumphantly at a row of small vials, "number one Chinese hero!"

"Hero?" said Ullis, and a warm yellow light switched on deep inside his brain, a forgotten node that had languished in darkness for a decade and more. "Yeah. I'll take a gram of the Chinese hero, heroine too if you have it."

"Bro," said Danny. "Don't say the H-word, okay? Cops here cool with C but they don't tolerate the other thing."

"Of course, forgive me, what was I thinking?" said Ullis, genuinely apologetic. "I'll take a gram of your finest h-dash-in."

Danny handed over a thin tapered vial of white powder. As Ullis put it carefully into his inside jacket pocket, Anis and the policeman walked into the projection room. The Romanian woman followed at a respectful distance like an obedient Indian wife, ten steps behind and eyes to the floor.

O, Romania, what have you become?

"Welcome," said Danny. "For what can I do you?"

Ullis moved to an armchair where he chopped a heroic Chinese line and heroically snorted it. There was no need to block his ears in tribute to the late Acharya Archie. The rush was instantaneous and nurturing, soft as the maternal breast. All of a sudden, the noonday tumult faded into the far background. He was hardly conscious of the people around him or of the sequence of events that had brought him to a basement bunker in the anterooms of hell. The rush spread in a slow unconditional wave from the back of his neck to his armpits and hips;

and from there to the fluid in his joints. He thought he heard a soft voice singing a children's song in Gujarati, a sweet call and response taken from an old playground melody. He had a question for Aki, if ever they were to meet again. He had a question for his wife, if only he could remember. But nothing could be ascertained above the voice in his head singing a song he had once loved in a language he didn't understand. It was a song she learnt as a child and taught him, along with the words for 'kiss', 'sweetness' and 'always'. She made a list of words and their translations in his notebook, which she had dated and signed. He remembered the melody, the comforting effortless lilt of it, but he had forgotten the words. Even so, it worked its healing properties, and he closed his eyes in gratitude. The question, what was the question he wanted to ask her? He almost had it when a vibration in his pocket brought him back. He opened his eyes on a scene of bilateral commerce, Anis putting a folded wad of notes into Danny's shimmering pouch. Ullis checked his phone. Payal was calling.

He picked up and said, "Let me call you back."

CHAPTER FIVE

She was about to run a bath when he called. She was watching CNN and sipping from a glass of Jim Beam on ice. Her suite had been the first in the hotel to have a television screen installed on the bathroom mirror. She was so taken with the idea that she got one on her dressing table mirror as well. Which made four screens in all, counting the flat screen mounted on the wall in the bedroom, slightly excessive by any reckoning. Why did she need so many televisions? What had she been thinking? Or perhaps she hadn't been thinking. Perhaps she'd been drinking. It wouldn't have been the first time.

At eleven in the morning, opening time, she'd asked Benny at the Harbour Bar to send her a bucket of his extra-large ice cubes that took ages to melt. Benny was the master of the all-important detail that made your alcohol experience immeasurably better and superior in every way to drinking at any bar other than the Harbour. He also sent up bitters and club soda and vermouth, everything except the single most important ingredient. Alcohol was forbidden to her because of certain untoward incidents in the past that she did not care to recall. It didn't matter that she owned (minuscule) shares in the hotel: she was banned from ordering anything remotely resembling a drinkie-poo. It infuriated her and so she devised a system. When friends came to visit she encouraged them to bring along a bottle or two, preferably Belvedere or

Beluga (though she was no snob when it came to distilled spirits and if there was no alternative she'd guzzle even the local rotgut, Romanov). In return she provided choice items from the room service menu.

At the moment she was willing to overlook the inconvenience of her predicament, that a grown grey-haired woman, mother to a grown son, was unable to order a drink in her private, not to say permanent suite. She was willing to let the resentment go, if only temporarily. The reason for her sunniness was this: she was feeling good for the first time in days, mellow, if that was the word. It had everything to do with the stuff she had found in her new friend's promotional Jim Beam backpack.

After he toddled off on his chore, she'd felt compelled to open the backpack and take a look inside. The white box had intrigued her – imagine, a backpack that held nothing more than a mid-sized box of powder – and she'd been further compelled, even duty-bound, to try an initial cautious line. It wasn't the best coke she'd ever had, and it certainly was not the worst, not by a long shot. She cut a few more lines, remarking at the lumpiness and strange colour. But she had enjoyed the effects, delicate and refined, as good as the best Colombian. Without a doubt it was designer stuff. She'd lucked out but she wasn't going to be greedy. She took a heaping tablespoon for herself and packed it safely in a baggie. The rest she left as she found it.

When the phone rang she said brightly, "Oh, hello!"

"Hello, it's me," said Ullis, inadvertently quoting Todd Rundgren.

"Where are you, darling?"

"On my way," he said, "mere moments away."

"Oh dear, I have to be off, Ulysses darling, to Alibag, which, as you know, is on the other side of the *globe*. I have a party to arrange. I'd love you to come along. Would you like to do that?"

"I don't see why n— yes, I'd like that."

"Only if you're back in time. Whatever shall I do with your backpack if you aren't?" She could leave it with the concierge. But what if they opened it? She had a bad enough reputation as it was.

"Count to ten and I'll be there," said Ullis urgently, "seriously, don't go without me."

Well then, she would wait until he returned. He sounded quite desperate, the poor man. She would settle on the couch and make herself another drink as she ran the bath – a little drinkie with a slow-melting Benny-inflected ice cube. And in the meantime she would try to unravel a mysterious tiny riddle. How had she become a woman who drank alone in hotel rooms in the middle of the day?

As a child she had watched her father start the morning with scotch. Mean with hangover, he would open a new bottle and take a first sip. He'd place the glass on the sink and only then would he brush his teeth. By the time he'd finished shaving, his famous charm was back in full force. The wolfish smile and kiss curl that the photographers adored. Master Raj was the life of the party again, the debonair son of the hotel's founder, the single father whose wife had left him less than a year into their marriage, the handsome playboy who managed to make even alcoholism seem glamorous. Sometimes he'd give her a sip because he liked to see the face she made. Doubtless this was the reason she'd developed a lifelong fondness for spirits of all kinds. She was eleven when he died of a heart attack in a hotel room in Geneva. As if in con-solation they had shipped her off to school in London, preceded by a year on the Continent where she stayed with her father's relatives or in hotels. She'd enjoyed the hotels because she'd made one of the great discoveries of her life, the minibar and its endlessly replenished tiny bottles of goodness. As a new student at SOAS she would take the occasional glass of wine. She switched to vodka around the time her politics hardened into activism. She protested on the streets. She cultivated and was cultivated by London's radical set. And she published an essay that suggested, via Marcuse and William Burroughs, that the internet was a form of social control. This was before social media became widespread. In some quarters her ideas were hailed as mildly prophetic, and she could have taken up a life in academia or publishing. Instead, she returned to India and resumed the ways of the idle heiress. Before she knew it she was drinking a bottle of vodka a day, starting with a jug of Bloody Mary that she made the night before and kept ready and waiting in the fridge.

She took her drink to the tub and watched the American president swing a golf club on CNN. He was not wearing a jacket and the enormity of his buttocks struck her anew. How could such a pear-shaped man with such an obese bum not be shamed every day of his life? If a duck-shaped woman were to be president she would be mercilessly trolled. She would be reminded constantly of her outsize bottom. Yet here was this man, this small-handed malignancy, swanning around the globe, golfing no less. Sick of the sight of him, she switched to a local news channel in which six people in six equal squares screamed at each other simultaneously. Not a word was comprehensible. Who were the screaming heads and what were they screaming about? She couldn't tell. But the pitch of the voices was unbearable and she hastily turned down the volume.

She took a sip of whisky and wondered why she watched television in the first place. Addicted. She was addicted to the stoppage

74

of linear time. When she allowed herself to be sucked into the screen, time dissolved into concept. It was like entering a new reality. The politicians and hucksters peddling slime and poison, the men in khadi and saffron who defended the indefensible, who protected the murderers acting in the name of the cow, who protected the rapists and the bullies.

She could not look away.

She watched as the scene switched to footage of the nation's bearded prime minister espousing yoga as a means to world peace. To demonstrate the truth of his assertion, he enacted a ridiculously simple asana that a novice could accomplish – by stretching his arms above his head. Oh, you silly man, she thought, you smug self-satisfied villain. Now he was blocking his nostril with a forefinger to demonstrate the correct breathing technique for the modern yogi. What earthly connection was there between him and the vast nation he so maliciously governed?

The very next piece of 'breaking' news was an old man being beaten up by a gang of teenage hoodlums for the crime of belonging to a religious minority. So here was the connection between the rulers and the ruled, between the tailored, barbered overlords and their unwashed foot soldiers. A plague of blood-gorged bloodsuckers battening on fear, a horde of upright leeches scouring the starving nation. Encased in fat, which they wore like armour, they divided the poor and mocked their poverty. They didn't worry about being held accountable for their crimes. Anything could be spun into a story about nationalism and its opposite. Equality was propaganda and reason was conspiracy and compassion a sign of weakness. What intoxicated them was power, the habit-forming rush of it, the way the masses parted and fell to genuflect in their presence. What drove them was sex, the ease of it, how easily it could be bought or coerced. For they were the new statesmen of India, all of them men, foul-mouthed and unlettered, squatting to eat, squatting to shit, squatting to watch porn in the houses of Parliament, stopping their convoys to piss squatting on the road – instigating, improvising, spreading. And what were they spreading? Exactly this: murder and the incitement to murder. The message was pounded home in the words they used and the words between the words. No image was too trite, no metaphor too laboured, no gesture too gross.

This was their great accomplishment. The way they hefted their testicles for reassurance that their genitals were intact, the way they touched themselves to make certain they were still men. But they were not men. They were blood-black humanoids with a taste for terror and sex. At their happiest when they were together, men without women, laughing, eating, yawning, cleaning their plates with their fat fingers. Cow-talk their preferred mode of communication, accomplished with much chewing of the cud, with much lowing and bellowing, with the endless proprietorial dropping of dung.

She watched with fascination and gratitude as the procession of the pitiless passed before her. Fascination, because that was the homage paid to power by the powerless. Was it not a privilege that she was even allowed to watch their craven enactments of perse-cution and revenge? And gratitude was due to the good lord for alcohol, because there was no other way to preserve one's sanity in the face of extreme yogic oppression.

Television. She couldn't look away.

She took a deep sip of bourbon and tasted smoke and comfort. Inevitably she thought of her father. What had he been doing in Geneva, of all places? Why was he alone? Was he alone? No one would tell her. When they brought the body back to India she'd not been allowed to see him. Her mother was a moderately well-known actress who had left her father soon after Payal was born. She had been in London making a movie. One morning she called Payal collect at the hotel.

"I'm so very sorry, darling Payal, but now you know why I left," she said, her voice muffled, as if it had to penetrate across many layers of cork and cotton wool.

"Why, Mummy?"

"Because he was such an old soak, darling, absolutely a tosspot."

"Will you stay in London for ever?" Payal asked.

"Of course not, my love," her mother said. "I'll be back just as soon as this wretched movie is finished. You know that. And now I must be off, Paolo's shooting me for *Vogue*. It's quite an honour as well as a tiny bit of a bore. Anyway, lots of love, darling."

She hadn't seen her mother since, which she supposed made her an orphan, a ward of the hotel, a bereft five-star princess. There are worse things, she'd told her eleven-year-old self, and gone right ahead with her life. She almost never missed her mother.

Now she splashed soapy water around the tub as more footage of the prime minister's yoga exercise was screened around the world. It called for urgent measures. She dried her hands and picked up her phone and sent a text message to a dozen numbers: "Tonight's the night! See you in Alibag, 8 p.m.! Be as late as you like!" Had she missed anyone? There was Feroze, to whom she owed money. If she didn't invite him, he would hear about it from mutual friends and her small window of opportunity would narrow even further. But she was willing to take this calculated risk. She would go out of her way not to see him. Who else? Her new friend Dom Ulysses, in the funereal black suit he refused to doff.

Did he own no other item of clothing? Or was it some kind of uniform, some indication of constant mourning?

She pulled the plug on the bath and rinsed with the hand shower and put on her navy blue robe. She called the butler service and asked for Imtiaz. When he arrived, she was in a pinstriped pantsuit putting the final touches on her eyes. She was sipping parsimoniously from a glass of water, no drugs or alcohol anywhere in her vicinity.

"Madam, good afternoon," said Imtiaz.

"Imtiaz, darling," she said, "I'm having some friends over tonight and I want you to pack a nice meal for about fifteen people."

"Certainly, madam," said Imtiaz, "what would you like as starters?"

"The poached scallops, I think? And the seared tuna and plenty of decent caviar with all the fixings."

She picked at a bowl of cut fruit and wiped her lips and applied a layer of nude Shanghai Spice. In the mirror she saw her father's brown eyes and healthy hair. As in her life, so in her face: no trace remained of her mother.

"Tenderloin and biryani for the mains?"

"Perfect. Also a selection of desserts, which I shall leave to you."

"Very good, madam. I will pack some handmade sorbets in ice. With crème brûlée and fruit?"

"Make sure there's nothing foamy, Imtiaz darling. I can't bear to *look* at foam, quite honestly," she said.

"Of course, madam."

"I'll be taking everything to Alibag, so pack it properly and put it in the car. *Will* that be all right, darling?"

"Right away, madam," said Imtiaz. "Shall I include linen and flowers?"

"No need at all."

"Will that be all, madam?" said Imtiaz, bowing as he left.

"I think so," she said, hearing the sound of traffic from the road below. She crossed the room to get her cigarettes from the coffee table and smoked an Esse standing at the big picture windows. They were digging up the walkway between the hotel and Apollo Bunder. Sometimes she heard bulldozers at odd hours of the night and early morning, and sometimes the sound of horse carriages taking customers for a truncated ride along the water because much of the road was closed to traffic.

From the window she saw bright sunlight on the bay and ferry boats plying to and from the Elephanta Caves. It was a peaceful view and it was unchanged for most of the year, except during the monsoons when everything disappeared under rain: her favourite season. First it wrapped the city in blankness. It destroyed the city then made it new. It remade the city in its own watery image. Bombayites believed only in what they could see and touch. Because they were always in the presence of water they knew they would become water molecules one day.

Her phone pinged: "Mom, don't forget to tell Mahesh to file before the 30th." It was Jack, all the way from London, reminding her to file her taxes. He knew she would forget otherwise. How had her son become so responsible at such an early age? What had she done right? Despite all the errors of her life, at least she had done this correctly. She had brought him up without mishap. Astonishing, considering how many dangers lay on the path between childhood and sense. How paranoid she had been each time he was out of her sight, how worried that some terrible accident would befall him. He had come out of it unscathed, a financial wunderkind, and nowadays he liked to parent his mum. She replied: "I will, darling. Skype me soon?"

On television the prime minister was cross-legged on a mat in the centre of a vast lawn, surrounded by people of all ages attempting the most basic of asanas. In her twenties and thirties she had practised hatha yoga for some years. At one time she had even been qualified to teach. Her criticism was professional as much as it was aesthetic. It was clear that the bearded man was play-acting. He was posing at posing and even this he didn't do correctly. It was the image that mattered, the great leader espousing yoga. It countered the hundreds of other images that clogged the screens and newspapers of the nation, the images of mutilation, of poor women dragged naked and screaming through the streets. On cue the screen cut to more footage of the old man being tortured by teenagers on the streets of Meerut, a godforsaken town in the lawless wastelands to the north of the nation, the old man pulled by his hennaed chin beard on a mud road, his attackers kicking him, hitting him with lathis, and what was this, were there policemen among them, clearing the way for the young thugs bent on blood? It was all too much. Television was the devil. This was why she couldn't look away. The devil would not let her.

She poured more bourbon and drank it down like medicine. She packed make-up, moisturiser, Mario Badescu buffering lotion and a small bottle of shampoo into a mesh pouch. She put the lot in a wheelie and added a pair of heels and a shawl. She switched channels to VH1. She hoped to find a Rihanna or Dua Lipa video. Instead there was Nicki Minaj, her second most favourite badass chick, rapping about ganja, rhyming "sex" with "ask", and "zen my body" with "lend my body". She turned it up loud enough to rattle the windows, and flipped through an interiors magazine.

When the doorbell rang, she felt strong enough to face whatever was on the other side. It was Dom Ullis at last, looking more malnourished than ever. How? Was it even possible? He seemed to have become skinnier and frailer in a matter of hours.

"So loud," he shouted. "The music."

"The remote's over there," she told him. "Under the *New Statesman*."

"*New Statesman*?" He stumbled over the Persian carpet as he moved the stack of magazines. "Now there's a name from the past."

"I still subscribe," she said. "Can't seem to shake the habit, I'm afraid. I'm so pleased you got here in the very nick of time."

He picked up the remote and turned the sound so low she could barely hear it. He took off his sunglasses. His eyes were huge and flecked with blood. "Sorry," he said. "Can't seem to take loud music, or advertisements, or gore in the movies. I used to love all that. Now I want pop music and Disney. I want rom-coms. What's wrong with me?"

"I don't think there's anything *wrong* with you," she said. "Something's right. You're embracing your inner maiden at last."

When he had made himself comfortable on the couch, she turned off the television and stood in front of him with her arms crossed. He was still apologising, earnestly, for turning down the music. She had no idea how to begin.

"Ulysses darling, I have to make a confession," she said.

"Good, good, so do I," said Ullis.

"Right then, you go first."

"My wife died. Her name was Aki. She was the editor of a publishing house. She loved loud music and she loved to dance. Suicide by hanging. I came home and found her. I think she wanted me to find her, to punish me. After the cremation I got on a plane and came to Bombay, because this used to be home for her. She grew up here and she always loved the city. I wanted to put her ashes into clean and flowing water the way you're meant to in the Hindu tradition. Delhi has no water except for the Yamuna, you know, the filthiest river in the world. I knew I'd have better luck in Bombay. I knew I'd find flowing water here, but I'm all out of luck. I'm out of the flow. Everything's wrong, I can see that. I'm no good without Aki. That's the simple truth. I'm no good and I want to hold on to her, to her ashes? I don't know, I don't know."

"You're carrying her ashes with you?" said Payal, as the full meaning of it came to her. "With you, *now*?"

"It's in the backpack, why I didn't want you to leave it here."

Silently, Payal had started to cry.

"I'm so sorry," she began. "But it was really good shit."

CHAPTER SIX

Why would a man leave a prized if disputed pair of chocolate loafers on a crud-encrusted road in suburban Bombay? If the dispute were with his (absent) wife, would he imagine her satisfaction at his newly entered state of shoelessness? Would he hear the ghostly echoes of a wifely tirade? *They don't suit you, the colour, the style, and most of all the feigned playboy insouciance. Take them off.* Would he or wouldn't he note the triumph in her tone? *I told you, crappy shoes!* The short answer: he surely would.

Just a few hours earlier, proudly loafered, Ullis had climbed into Payal's midnight blue Range Rover. The driver wore a white uniform and peaked cap. He took the car on the scenic route north, past Marine Drive and Wilson College and Worli, the sea to the left of them, chaos to the right. At first they exchanged a few words, but as the car entered the city's congested central precincts Payal and Ullis fell silent, like old friends or family members who were talked out and talked through. Or like a married couple joined by name and circumstance and the brute force of years spent together, with no reason to speak over the cacophony of the street. He was grateful for the silence. More and more he thought it better not to speak. Why bother when it caused only confusion or misery? Better to communicate like the animals – only with the eyes and the body, only with sparse curated cries. Better to save one's words for the birds. At least they could be trusted to be true to themselves.

Stalled on the Haji Ali seafront in a crush of luxury cars and battered black-and-yellow taxis, he saw a juice shop he had known in the days of opium. Like many landmarks in the city, a low wall of metal police barricades cordoned off the sidewalk in front. You could no longer park by the sea wall and order a chikoo shake or strawberry cream. You waited in your car and grabbed your takeaway carton and fled for dear life. Except life was not dear. It was cheap. It was cut-rate, discounted, quickly consumed and easily returned. Living in the new Bombay was like living in a medieval town under siege. You knew sooner or later there would be another attack, or riot, or flood. You knew the end of the world was coming and you took it in your stride. You had no other choice.

Beside the juice shop was a walkway that led across a short stretch of sea to the Haji Ali dargah. He couldn't see it for the smog but he knew it was there, and his memory, enhanced by distance and time, rendered the monument more clearly than in life, each detail magnified into myth: the broken concrete of the walkway on the sea, the narrow tapered length of it, the way the minarets appeared before you at high tide, as if they were resting on whitecaps.

After a pipe or several pipes at Rashid's opium shop, Archie, Hormazd and Ullis had once walked from Shuklaji Street to Haji Ali, all the way from the city's unwashed underworld to the districts of gold and glass. Then, purely for the stoned whim of it, they'd taken the walkway to the tomb of the Uzbekistani merchant and Sufi saint who had settled in these parts when the city was little more than seven malarial islands at the edge of the Arabian Sea. According to Hormazd, the saint, a Pir known as Ali, had asked to be buried at sea because he didn't want to burden the earth with his remains. Humility, possibly false, or a wish to step lightly, to leave no mark. When Ali died some of his followers cast the coffin into deep water, but it drifted back to shore at Worli. They built a monument at the spot, a tomb of floating Mughal minarets clustered around a humble white dome. When seen from a distance, the pillars and arches seemed to hang wavering on the water.

The kilometre-long route was difficult to navigate on a clear day. That afternoon the sea had been rough and the entire length of the walkway was crowded with the blind and the maimed. The air soft and moist, hanging to your arms like wool. Destitute pilgrims sitting with their begging bowls on both sides of the path, wealthier pilgrims walking among them to the dargah. Shrivelled men and women with shrivelled infants in their arms. Day-tripping gawkers. It made the walkway an obstacle course of constant foot traffic. For Archie and Ullis there was an added difficulty, two hits each of Mandrax, a drug that made walking unpredictable even on a smooth surface. They progressed slowly, with many stops and starts, drunken sailors on a storm-tossed schooner.

"Listen, fuckface," Archie said, using his standard mode of address in those days. "I wanna give these poor choothiyas some wigwam. What can you spare?"

Hormazd couldn't spare a penny. He wasn't strolling for his health. He was on foot because he was poor. "If I had the money," he said softly, "I would take a fucking taxi."

"Gimme," said Archie. "Whatever you can."

Reluctantly Hormazd parted with two one-rupee notes and half a handful of change.

"Solid," said Archie. "What about you?"

"Certainly not," said Ullis, whose lips and legs were pleasantly rubbery. It was the best part of the Mandrax buzz, the moment when the ricochet took you over and turned the world into a pleasing, passing blur. The elastic in your limbs made it difficult to stay upright for any length of time, which meant you had to give up all attempts at motor control. The result was nothing less than liberation from the dictatorship of the senses. Soon it would be difficult to talk and impossible to think. "I'm not going to insult them with pennies. If you can't give something substantial I'd say keep walking."

This stopped Archie for a moment.

"You arrogant bastard," he said. "Got to be the supreme fuck-face in a community of fuckfaces, isn't that right?"

Jerkily he put together whatever small notes and coins he had mustered, about three rupees in all, and gave it to a girl who sat with her blind parents on mats near the water. No older than six or seven, she held a baby in her arms. A child holding a child. She examined Archie's offering with interest. Then she laughed and shook her head and returned the money.

"Please take it," Archie said.

The girl refused.

"Please," said Archie, begging the beggar.

She got up and dusted the mat on which she'd been sitting, the baby on her hip, absorbed in folding and putting away her family's few belongings.

"Please," Archie said again, holding out the money. "Take. It's for you."

Ullis took his friend by the elbow and led him in the direction of the dargah, but Archie pulled roughly away and went back to the girl, who refused even to look at him. Finally, made stupid by frustration, he placed the money on the ground in front of her. A mistake.

"Chal, gandu," the girl said. In the strangeness of the moment even the grown-up curse word seemed well chosen, attracting the attention of some of the other beggars, who stopped their chanting for the moment. "Gandu," she said again in her old man's voice, and then she put a small hand on his chest and pushed.

Archie lurched backwards, flailing his arms in an effort to keep his balance, and for a moment it seemed he might succeed but then he fell sideways to the narrow strip of land. His glasses flew off his head and landed in his lap. Ullis had never seen his friend's eyes in their nakedness, golden eyes, defenceless in the clear light from the water. Somehow he had managed to fall without tumbling into the sea. Elegantly splayed across the walkway in his dirty white kurta and white pyjamas, he looked very much like the men and women and children who squatted there professionally, who appeared punctually each morning as if they were clocking in at a corporate job. They too wore white kurtas, the uniform of the professional beggar, and because he was dressed as they were, they regarded him now with open hostility. A place on the walkway was a prized source of income allotted according to a strict system. Archie was angled across the middle of it, while an impatient line of pilgrims formed on either side. Soon they'd begin to complain and so would the beggars. In minutes the scene would turn ugly. There would be broken teeth and blood spatter on the rocks, like drops of rain before a storm. It was inevitable.

How would they kick against the pricks? Archie and Ullis were rubbery on Mandrax and hopelessly opiated. In a word: beautiful. Also: outnumbered. They stood no chance against a sober horde of professionals. And where was Hormazd while this drama

87

played out? There, hurrying in the middle distance, already half-way to the road. Retreat, good fellows, thought Ullis, as he picked up his fallen friend and limped past the gauntlet of angry faces on both sides of the path. All the way, Archie complained.

Twenty-five years later the city had barricaded itself, but its essential feature had not changed. All along the Range Rover's route were loiterers, men mostly but also women, smoking or eating or chewing paan. They strolled or perched on the wall and stared vacantly at the passing traffic. Today, the city seemed to be full of people reeling from one catastrophe and steeling themselves for the next.

In that sense he was almost lucky. Almost. No catastrophe could be worse than the one he had already endured. Nothing will harm me again, he reminded himself for the hundredth time. It had come to pass, the thing he most feared: his wife dead by her own hand. She had hinted at it from their first meeting, as if to let him know he had been fairly warned. He told her about his progressive condition and she had said, just as flippantly, that she had one too. The words she'd used were so simple and so terrible there could be no reply.

Regret is the river of the world.

For most of the four years they were together, he and Aki had survived on their salaries. They had skimped without saving. They lived small. Four months before her death, his parents had begun to send him the monthly income from a property owned by the family. It had been a gift of freedom that came too late. If only he had known how limited their time together would be, what would he have done? What would he not have done? And what would it have changed?

He remembered the multitudes of meaning the word *low* held for Aki. If he asked what she'd been doing all day she would say, "I was low." As if it were a full-time job. If he asked where she'd been she'd say, "I've been low." As if it were a republic to which she had a multiple-entry twenty-year visa. Or she would say, "Listen, sunshine, I better warn you, the low is coming. I can feel it." Once he had suggested they take a weekend trip out of Delhi and she'd said, "I can't do it tomorrow, I'm going to the low." As if her low country lay everywhere like a vast spiritual archipelago.

The low was most dangerous when it coincided with her periods, the physically torturous episodes that stretched sometimes for a week. She experienced cramps and crippling pain, when she could do little more than lie in bed with a hot water bottle pressed to her tummy. She had killed herself on the day her period began. It was as random and contingent as that. If it had been any other day, any other hour, it would not have happened. He remembered times when her mood would capsize for no reason at all. The time she refused to speak or leave the house for days. The time she disappeared without a word. After an hour or two he called and heard her cell phone ringing in the bedroom. She returned six hours later without a word of apology or explanation. Instead there were accusations. Why had he not tried to find her? She was at Humayun's Tomb. She'd been sitting on a bench, waiting for him. Why had he not thought of it? She ignored his anguished protestations, that he had not known where she was, that he was not clairvoyant, that he had been worried out of his mind. The worst period-related episode happened soon after he told her that his condition, hepatitis C, was blood-borne and they had to be careful. He'd found her in the bathroom one afternoon, shaving her legs with his razor.

"What are you doing?"

She stopped her work and looked up at him, her eyes brilliant and distant.

"You mustn't . . ." he began.

"Don't worry," she'd said. "Nothing will happen."

This was her slogan. There was no need to worry because nothing would happen. She was fearless when it came to physical danger and it was only after her death that he came to understand why.

Once, in an airplane, because he was bothered by the turbulence, she said: "You don't really think you're going to die like this, do you? After surviving everything you've survived you're not going to die in some random stupid accident."

"That's exactly how people die," he'd replied.

She had said nothing, merely giving him a look, her expression the precise equivalent of, 'Pshaw!' Then, going back to the rom-com she'd been watching, she said, "You're a very silly boy, Dommie."

It was her name for him. Nobody else called him this. She pronounced it with a high peculiar inflection, both syllables stressed equally in a child's sweet monotone. It always stopped him mid-sentence. Everything was made all right with just the one word.

Who would call him Dommie again?

To never hear your voice, except in dreams. To never see you again, except in dreams. Or at an airport, from a distance, knowing it isn't you.

Nothing frightened her, not violence or the threat of danger, not isolation or intimidation or physical injury. He understood it now. Much too late, he understood. Aki's fearlessness was the result of simple deduction: compared to her own fantasies of dying, the dangers posed by the real world were irrelevant, banal, not worth worrying about. The world's horrors would never match the horrors in her head.

Ullis believed Aki might have approved of Payal. They might have been friends. They might even have had a mother-daughter bond. Aki would not have minded being snorted in error by the kleptomaniacal Payal. She would have liked the idea of her ashes entering the living waters of another's body. When Payal told him she had looked in his backpack and found the box and assumed it was drugs – because after all it was such a small box, and who would imagine that a person could fit into such a tiny container – he had not known what else to do but tell her it was okay, it wasn't her fault, how was she to know? He had ended up comforting her when he was the one in need of comforting.

He was beginning to realise that this was the true meaning of grief: comfort flowed in the reverse direction. Outwards it went from the grief-stricken, in ever-widening circles, first to close relatives and friends and neighbours, then to distant relations, acquaintances, foes, the unknown faces that floated up out of the dark. Comfort travelled in one direction only. There was no return gift.

They were passing the turn-off to the airport, which meant they had left the near suburbs and would soon be among the unerringly strange place-names, in Chinchpokli, Titwala, Bhandup and Khopoli, far-flung locations he had never visited and would never visit except possibly in a state of drug-induced madness.

But this was an unfair smear against the suburbs. As the bards of Brooklyn and the poets of Paterson had proved, even the unassuming address was a fit setting for literachure. Why couldn't there be a collection of epic poems and fairy tales titled, *Chinchpokli & Other Stations of the Cross*? Or a seven-part Proustian memoir, *My Malad, My Wadala*? Or a mystifying exercise in cinéma vérité, *Dombivli, Mon Amour*?

On the highway, traffic flowed freely. Air was another matter. The sun had disappeared behind layers of dense smog and particulate matter, smog so sensuous it felt like fur against the skin. He tasted the unmistakable tang of chemicals. Was it an emanation from his pores, a side effect of the bastardly meow, or one more layer of the city's thousand-layered miasma? Possibly it was the meow because the chemicals tasted sweet to his tongue.

"Could we stop somewhere for a minute?" he said. "A pit-stop for the brain and bladder?"

"Bharat, take us to Lila Palace," Payal told the driver immediately, as if she had been hoping for just such a request. Soon they pulled up at an iron gate and turned into a circular driveway. There was the usual sequence of obstacles, the uniformed turbaned doormen, the wand frisk, the grand staircase and the revolving door.

"Come with me, darling," said Payal.

Ullis went with her. What is it about me that makes people say that? Is it something in my face, some naked thing crying out for direction? Because I hear it once a day at least, and every time I hear it I am strangely compelled to obey.

As they stepped into the lobby Payal was accosted by a young woman in a purple-and-lime sari, whose face glowed with excitement. It was the face of the acolyte meeting the object of her devotion. Her rapt expression reminded him of something, or someone.

"Madam Payal," she said. "Madam Payal, do you remember me?"

"I'm not quite *sure*, darling, though I must say you look very nice. Did we get drunk somewhere?"

The young woman's face crumpled into picturesque distress.

"Oh no!" she said, horrified. "I worked in your hotel at the reception desk. Three months! Once I helped you to your room and you gave me a bottle of perfume. Issey Miyake!"

"Ah, you're very welcome, child."

"Madam Payal, what can I do for you? Please let me help you in some way? It would be my honour."

"Sweetie, we are here simply for a bit of peace and quiet. I want to look at your lawns for a moment."

"I will take you," said the woman – and Ullis remembered. The expression on her face, the open admiration when she looked at Payal, it was identical to Jennifer's at the coffee shop of the Taj.

"No, my dear, you will *not*. You must stay at your station where I have no doubt you are doing a wonderful job. You must leave us to our solitude."

After some persuasion, the woman agreed to let Payal find her own way to the outside seating area.

"Bye, sweetie," Payal said as she left, and to Ullis: "Why are the young in this country so eager to prostrate themselves at the altar of wealth and old age? Are they born with a love of the whip, do you think, or is it an acquired taste?"

She led the way through a landscaped garden to wide lawns bordered by palm trees. There were wrought-iron tables and sun umbrellas. There was a pond and a hump-backed bridge.

She pointed at a flagstone path leading to a bamboo grove and a group of tile-roofed buildings. It was all so picturesque and heartbreaking, Aki's favourite kind of landscape: green lawns, a small body of water, no roses anywhere.

"The facilities," said Payal, "are thataway. I'll see you back here."

He walked splay-legged on the widely spaced flagstones, his eyes on the chocolate loafers he had bought against the wishes of his wife. "No," she had insisted, "absolutely not. They're old man's shoes, don't do it." But he had done it. He had bought them and worn them every chance he got. Truth be told she was right, they *were* old man's shoes. But he'd always enjoyed her expression of annoyance when she saw them.

In the bathroom he ignored the attendant and went into a cubicle, where he hung up his jacket and found the drugs and considered his immediate options. For now he had the vial of heroin and the bag of cocaine. He could mix the two and cut a substantial line that would keep him going until they got to Alibag, wherever in the world that was. But the heroin would lead inevitably to the kingdom of the low, a shining city in a valley unmarred by the presence of humans. Heroin demanded solitude. He preferred to visit there on his own. Buoyed by virtuousness, Ullis put away the vial of H and made a medium-fat line of the clean and subtle and infinitely varied cocaine. After a moment's consideration he augmented the initial foray with another. When he emerged from the cubicle, he gave his jacket to the attendant and rolled up his sleeves. He cupped shaky hands and splashed water on his face and made it a point not to look at his reflection in the multiple mirrors.

Payal sat at a wrought-iron table shielded by an oversized umbrella. Her round sunglasses were perched on top of her head like an extra pair of insect eyes. She was watching a video on her phone. Ullis heard a deadpan woman's voice rapping about ganja and heartache. He could hardly believe it. Payal was a rap-head like Aki. Did nobody listen to other kinds of music any more?

"Darling! You take longer than some ladies I know," Payal said when he returned, her eyes on her phone.

"Thank you, Madam Payal," he responded obsequiously.

"Just one second," she said. "I love the end of this Nicki Minaj vid. Did you know she was born in Trinidad like that *awful* V. S. Naipaul?"

"I did not know that, no," said Ullis, marvelling briefly at the flatness of the world. "I'll try not to hold it against her."

Then they were back in the Range Rover and back on the road. They overtook a truck stocked with bullocks miserably squeezed together on the flatbed trailer. The animals wobbled heavily from side to side, black flanks wet and streaked with mud. They passed metro construction and stopped at a bottleneck. As they turned onto the highway he felt his pulse accelerate. His eyes, he knew, were abnormally bright. A lava lamp of butter-flies migrated from his stomach to his chest. The cocaine was so clean and uncut even the rush was on a time release. Grinding his teeth, he wiped the sweat from his head and looked wildly at the endless road and the snarling infinite traffic. Almost imme-diately there was a clamour within.

He said, "Sorry, could we stop? I really do need to pee."

"Again? Well what *were* you doing at the Lila? Oh never mind, you don't have to answer that," said Payal.

They crossed an intersection and pulled over near a pay-to-play toilet.

"Wait, here?" said Ullis dubiously, eyeing the grubby entrance.

"Yes, here," said Payal, "welcome to Bombay, Ulysses darling. We no longer have to pee on the street."

There was no way around it. Taking a deep breath, he stepped out of the car and directly into a flattened pile of dung. What kind of dung, human, bovine, elephantine, alien? There was no way to tell. He stood still for a moment and weighed possible avenues of retreat, one foot in the shit, one wavering above. Then, gingerly, he walked into the toilet. He peed into a trough and paid the attendant and returned to the car, examining throughout his once-pristine chocolate loafer now encased in mystery dung. There was no way he could smuggle his shoes into Payal's automotive showpiece. He would wrap them in newspaper and put them in the boot and attempt later to hose them down. But as soon as the thought occurred he knew he would not actually do it, hose down a pair of shoes. His course of action was exceedingly clear. The footwear must be jettisoned, discarded, given up, abandoned forthwith. Somewhere the spirit of Aki was smiling, if not dancing the I-told-you-so hula. As Dominic Ullis left the caked loafers on the road and stepped barefoot into the shitless interiors of the Range Rover, he heard his wife's low voice. Very distinctly, making no effort to temper her glee, Aki said, *Crap shoes!*

CHAPTER SEVEN

She had always been subject to vivid dreams that spilled into her waking life and left her slow in the morning, stunned and silent for an hour or more. When she told her husband her dreams, he did little to disguise his disinterest. To him dreams held no significance. They were residue, like cigarette ash or litter, incidental items left over from the day. He told her not to speak about dreams, except to those she trusted most, because dreams exposed you. Now she was dead her dreams were more vivid than they had been when she was alive. Which was no surprise. Death was a transfer of consciousness, a change of costume. Nothing more. She'd prepared for it all her life. And in the final minutes, after she stepped from the desk and felt the dupatta bite into her neck, not even then had she changed her mind. Her will had taken over. Suspended from the fan while the chiffon tightened and her vision exploded and her face was seeded with a hundred red blooms, even then she had not changed her mind. It was afterwards, when it was over and nothing could be changed, that was when she knew she had made a mistake. Regret came in increments like the drip of a tap improperly closed.

Confined to the vicinity of the box in which her ashes had been placed, her dreams ran free of temporal matters. She no longer concerned herself with the boredom of housekeeping and employment, the disappointing machinations of a social life, her husband's precarious hold on sobriety and sanity. Free of encumbrance, she circled around a single mystifying vision.

She was on foot, alone on a road of yellow dust. There were no fields or houses, just the road bordered by trees, the old dusty trunks numbered in red and white paint. She was holding a canteen and she took a small sip, no more, to wet her lips. There wasn't much water left and she didn't know how much further she would have to walk. Even inside the dream she knew she was dead. Her body and its million interlocking parts no longer belonged to her. Not that this made things easier. True knowledge of the world and its requirements persisted in the region of her upper abdomen. The body was no longer hers but she was still its subject: she needed water and she felt fatigue. Fear was a constant. She was done with the body but it would not let her be.

When she saw the small figure sitting on a culvert by a milestone, she did not slacken. She looked at the slow-motion drift of her feet on the road and it seemed so far away. She resolved not to look at him but he was waving at her with both hands.

"Howling," said the backlit figure, speaking in a child's high voice, his features indistinct. "I'm crippled and half blind. I'm small and light. Carry me on your back a little way and I *will* reward you. I promise, handsomely you will be rewarded!"

Aki considered his neediness and disability. She considered her new state. How disembodied she was, yet how conscious of the body. How long would it last, the new consciousness? And once it was gone would she be gone too? She would make use of her corporeality, even if only for as long as the dream lasted.

She let the dwarf-like figure climb on her back and realised her mistake. He was unaccountably heavy. He slowed her down and he had a terrible way of patting her on the head as if she were a pony or a cow. Dizzy from exertion and thirsty again, she stopped for a moment and sat on a culvert.

"What are you doing?" he screamed. "We have a long way to go. Go on! All I ask is that you go on! If you're not true to your purpose, what are you?"

She got up, not because she was afraid of him, but because she couldn't bear his high-pitched baby voice. As she walked, the cripple's heels dug into her ribcage. He kept patting her head with his calloused hand. With each pat he seemed to get heavier. She fell to her knees, her bones as brittle as glass. I am breaking up. Aren't I breaking into a million red pieces?

"Get up," screamed the cripple. "You can't stop here. You don't know what lies ahead and you have no idea what is behind. Keep going, that's your job. There's nothing else you have to do."

"One minute," she said, "just one minute, let the poor horse catch her breath."

She turned her head for a glimpse of the tight small figure lodged on her back. Time had passed and night was falling. He made a gesture that was lost in the dusk.

"Do your work," he screeched. "Don't you understand? Do what you're supposed to and everything will follow."

He bucked his heels into her as if she were a misbehaving mule. He kicked into her sides but she felt the strain in her spine. She staggered forward and stopped, swaying on her feet. She needed water, but where was the canteen?

Her eyes failed her then and she fell a long way to the road.

When she came to, it was dark. The moon was low and red and translucent. She got to her feet and walked a little, slow from the dizziness. Ahead of her a small malevolent shape moved rapidly, drinking from a canteen. He was drinking her water and he could walk just fine! Rage overcame her. The hot wire tightened her brain and rendered her blind and unafraid.

She caught up with him and saw his face up close, his full profile and the intensely familiar shape of his head. It took her a moment to register the round face and full cheeks, the weak eyes, the lips unused to smiling. A taste of metal rose in her throat. It was her own face, exaggeratedly enhanced, unhappier than she had thought possible.

She noticed that the landscape was empty, as if it had been picked clean by carrion birds. On the side of the road an uprooted milestone lay flat. She picked it up with her powerful hands and smashed the dwarf on his head, again and again until her hands were sticky and the stone slipped from her grasp. She took the canteen from his hands and tipped its meagre contents into her mouth.

It was then that she heard the terrible noise of angels, dozens of them, their great swollen wings dragging on the ground, surrounding her with a forest of black shapes and sleek dog bodies. They stood on their hind legs and their wings breathed like living fur. Tears fell from their eyes.

One among them stepped forward and admonished her in words she strained to follow. He picked up the small body and lifted it in his arms and said: YOU killed him. What punishment shall equal YOUR crime?

"Who is he?" she asked.

But the angel wept so piteously he did not hear.

"Tell me," she said. "Who is he?"

And she put her hand on the angel and beseeched him.

The angel stopped weeping long enough to say one name.

Since her death she had circled around the same set of images and the same dream, if it was a dream: the moment she stepped from the desk into the noose of the dupatta, the way her legs moved of their own accord, scissoring and locking, the moment the struggle ceased, the dream of the dwarf that came to her, the disembodied body that was her new state, here not here, accompanying her husband on his flight from Delhi, watching him, a man adrift in his own waking dream, addicted to gestures without meaning or intent. She knew why he had left Delhi. He was afraid of touching those things to which memories were attached. How foolish he was! To think there was anything in the world that was unencumbered by memories. By not touching her things, by not sleeping in their bed, by cutting himself off, he hoped to put himself out of reach of the past. He hoped to freeze himself in place. He hoped to be as dead as she. He didn't understand that he *must* touch her by touching the things that had belonged to her. He didn't realise that everything she was, the breath and breadth of her life, now had passed to him.

She was beholden to speak to him. But how? In any case, this impulse too was residue. She did not have to follow through. How did it matter? Not long ago it had mattered terribly. Now everything had changed. Stripped of urgency, everything that had seemed important was revealed at last in its true aspect. Her grief at being abandoned as a child and left for months with an aunt; her reinvention of herself as a school bully, who exacted from the weaker students a daily payment of fear or obeisance; her first love affair, in graduate school in Florida, with a boy who was engaged to someone else, whose wedding she helped to organise; her own marriage to a man she hardly knew, plunging into it without caution or consideration; her education, her career, the accumulation of objects, the paying of taxes, keeping account of income and expenditure – all of it insignificant, hieroglyphs on sand, old concerns that slipped from her like garments she no longer wore.

Even the last argument with her husband, which had seemed hopeless at the time, came to her now like a scene from a play whose premise she couldn't remember, a scene in which actors simulated anger while negotiating Delhi's murderous traffic.

He was driving her to the office as usual, as he had done for a year, to the Connaught Place high-rise where she worked.

"I'm done with working here," she'd said. "I'm not doing it any more. I've been meaning to tell you but I don't know how to say it."

"Just say it the way you do."

"They're hiring someone new that I'll have to report to."

She was shaking her head and she wouldn't look at him. She knew what he was going to say and she resented it already. He had no right.

"It might not be so bad," he said. "Might even be good, someone to share the responsibility? How can you decide you hate it before it's happened?"

She stared at the traffic and refused to look at him.

"You don't get it," she said, quietly, hopelessly. "I've been the boss and they're hiring a new boss. Someone I don't want to work with. It's finished here. I want to start my own publishing house."

"If it were that easy to start a business . . ." said her husband. "Don't rush into a decision."

"I've already decided."

"Let's think about it for a minute. Remember how hard you worked to get this job."

They were stuck in eight lanes of traffic around the India Gate. Ahead of them a driver had got out of his car to yell at a motorcyclist. A traffic policeman had arrived to make things worse. Her husband tried to reverse but it was impossible. On either side of them cars honked and idled. A pall of smoke hung over everything.

She hadn't seen the sky in weeks. She had forgotten there were stars above them. It was as if an impenetrable veil had fallen between her and the heavens. She couldn't imagine why people lived like this. For what reason did they submit to it? Surely there were alternatives? Unrelievedly ugly men and women surrounded by unrelieved ugliness. This was the truth of the city. All around her the mean minds idled in their pollution machines. There was not a face she could like. In the midst of it all, she and her husband, fighting, wretched, undistinguished.

"I'm red meat," she said. "Someone's done for, don't you see who it is?"

"What?"

"If meat is my destiny why don't you see it in my face? You're my husband."

"Why are we talking about destiny and meat?"

"I can't do it any more. I can't allow myself to be bullied. It's horrible to work for someone you don't admire and hope never to resemble. Whatever happens, I'm quitting," she said.

"So why are we having this conversation if you've already decided," said her husband in the tone he used when he was angry, the condescending, withering tone that made her feel like a worthless child.

She let her frustration show. In a controlled monotone she told him she had expected better, she had expected him to be supportive. She had not thought he would question something so important, so fundamental to her wellbeing and mental health. She spoke without once raising her voice. She told him he had exceeded his responsibility as her husband and fallen short at the same time. He had no right to tell her what to do when he knew what the alternative would cost. If this was the way he was going to respond to a crisis, by telling her not to do anything, by saying she should keep it going because that was the comfortable thing to do, because there were bills to pay and they needed her salary, well then, there was hardly any point in being together. She went on in this way for five or ten minutes. He tried to interject at first and then he fell silent. She noticed how badly he was driving, grinding the gears and leaning on the horn. She was still talking when he made his outburst.

"Stop, stop, or I'll crash the car," he'd said, surprising only himself. She liked the idea. It was something that had occurred to her. What if they were to die together in a crash, or fall from a tall building, or succumb to a gas leak in the kitchen? Together. Die as they lived. Wouldn't it solve all their problems at once?

But they made it to the office in one piece, crash-free, still alive. Even as she left the car and gathered her handbag and phone, she refused to look at him. She didn't say goodbye or kiss him. She took the elevator up to the eighteenth floor and walked past the empty reception desk and fled into her office, where she sat on the couch for five minutes with her head in her hands. Then work had taken over. She'd put aside one set of frustrations and taken up another. A shipment of books had gone missing. The receptionist called in sick and an intern had to fill in. There was a shortfall in the petty cash box. There was a call from New York for which she had had to sound energetic and intelligent. She just about managed intelligent. There was a meeting with the distributors, strapping Delhi boys who spoke not a word of English and seemed only slightly put off that a woman was in charge. There was copy to write and copy to reject. There was a phone call with an author, handholding and reassurances on her part, anxiety and whining on his. And there was nothing unusual about any of this, the routine crises of a Monday morning; but in her head something had shifted, she could feel it, a change in the weather.

At lunch she and Amung ordered Mughlai from Ranjit da Dhaba. As usual Amung asked impossibly intimate questions. As usual Aki painted her husband in the best possible light.

"How often does he kiss you?"

"Every day," she said truthfully.

"How often do you sleep?"

Aki squeezed lime on the cut onions and sprinkled salt and pepper.

"Everybody sleeps, Amung," she said teasingly. "I try to sleep every night. Don't you?"

"Not like that, yaar, Aki. You know what I mean. How often do you *sleep*?"

"Not every night like we used to, but often enough."

"How often?"

"Every other night and first thing in the morning."

"Hemant is the same. Morning is the best time, he says, when you're fresh and all. Is he good, your hubby?"

"What a funny word, Amung. Hubby. Yes he's good, a proper gentleman. He always lets me go first."

"No!"

"Always."

"Hemant is not so considerate, but."

"Never marry a man under the age of thirty-three," said Aki.

"They aren't like us. They're handicapped and, what's the word, stunted."

"Stunted?"

"Yes. They take longer to develop into thinking adults and sometimes it never happens. Go for older. At least then they take a bit of time. It's a minimum requirement, time and talent. You should insist on it, in my opinion."

"How much time he takes?"

"Hours. He says things to prolong it."

"Hemant also says things. 'Oh God, yes baby yes,' he'll say. Repeats himself, *yes, yes, yes*, like he won the lottery."

"Dom says poetry."

"What do you mean?"

Aki watched Amung's lovely eyes widen in alarm.

"He says poems, recites poems from memory," she said. "Sometimes it will put me off. Not sexy, I tell him. He says that's the point. The words pull you back from the brink and start you over."

"Like? I want to hear. Please tell."

"Now? Over chicken dopiaza and butter naan? Before ice cream? Before coffee?"

"Tell!"

"There's one that starts like this: *Rose, thou art sick, the invisible worm that flies in the night in the howling something, something.* I said, Dom, are you calling me a sick rose? You know I don't like roses. I think they're boring and obvious and only boring and obvious people like them."

"Better to be a sick rose than an invisible worm flying in the night."

"You know, Amung, I never thought of it in that way. You're right.

There's a chance the sick rose may get better. Invisible worms are invisible for ever."

Amung stopped chewing and gave Aki a look of appraisal.

"What did *he* say?"

"He said, you may be a sick rose but you're my sick rose."

"Aki. So sweet!"

She was surprised she still remembered these things. The pull of emotion was gone but she remembered everything. The look on Amung's face, like a snapshot curling slightly at the edges. The smell in the conference room, of food and flowers. She remembered but she took no sides. Her feelings didn't get in the way of her memories. Nothing remained but the relief of distance and a recollection of what it meant to be alive: the need to communicate, even if the need lessened consecutively and waned like the light at the end of day.

She would find a way to talk to him.

CHAPTER EIGHT

When you're high, time dissolves like powder in a spoon. It melts and bends to your will. When the high is gone, time returns in the company of boredom to punish you with the time you killed.

It had been no more than twenty minutes since Ullis's sojourn at the toilet of the Lila, where he had weighed the benefits of cocaine versus heroin and decided to postpone the reward of H until later. He had never done such a thing, scored heroin and not ingested it immediately. Like all junkies, he knew that gratification delayed was gratification denied. But he *had* done it, firmly and virtuously. He'd just said no. Instead he'd snorted a fat, if not obese, line of cocaine, which put a shimmer in his head, a hurt on his nose and a grind inside his teeth. It was blissful and now it was gone. Only twenty minutes had passed since that essential nasal intervention and he was already in the market for another. Either the cocaine was not as good as he had thought or his tolerance was increasing from one snort to the next. He looked forward to it, incremental leaps, ruinous progression, a mathematical dance unto death.

"I say, Payal?"

"Yes, darling, of course you can borrow a pair of slippers when we get to the house."

"No, no, I mean yes, but the thing is, I was wondering if we could make one more stop, a last one for the road? I think it's going to be one of those days."

"Look, is this about, like, powdering your nose? Because we don't need to stop for that, you know, Ulysses darling. I mean, if you haven't noticed? The windows are *tinted*?"

"And what about . . . ?" said Ullis, inclining his head in the direction of the driver.

"Bharat?" There was a throaty laugh. "He's not going to mind, are you, Bharat?"

"No, madam," said Bharat, his eyes meeting Ullis's in the rear-view mirror. Under his peaked white cap the driver's hair was the same shade of silver as his mistress's. Was it a prerequisite for gainful employment with Madam Payal?

"Bharat used to work for the government, didn't you, Bharat?"

"Yes, madam, garment of India."

"Ah," said Ullis, who had once delighted in the linguistic excesses of his countrymen, "and why did you shed the garment and turn to other forms of cover?"

"Why do you think?" said Payal. "Because the pay is better. Also darling, don't be mean to the servants? Bharat, turn up the AC. It's *so* warm. Don't you think so?"

Bharat turned up the AC and opened a console near the front seat. He passed to the back a square mirror. Somehow he managed to accomplish this without taking his eyes off the road, currently a broken stretch that teemed with cars and handcarts, scooters and autos, dogs and pedestrians and a sedate shaggy camel.

"Thank you," said Ullis, momentarily uplifted by the unexpected resourcefulness of the fellow in the peaked cap. Before the black maw returned to suck on his brain and spit out the husk, he got to work. He dropped a small rock on the mirror, and flattened and chopped it with some adept wielding of his debit card. Fashioning two lines, he offered the mirror to Payal with a rolled-up note.

"God," she said, "I was *beyond* mortified, beyond, that I snorted your ashes, I mean your wife's ashes. Gutted! And now I feel *so* connected to her, like, seriously, bonded. Still and all I *am* sorry, darling, honestly, I can't apologise enough."

She snorted both lines and passed the mirror back.

Ullis crushed the rest of the rock. Inspired by Victor's precision work, he made three tiny lines that he vaporised with a rapid back and forth movement of the note.

Payal had indeed seemed mortified when he told her what she had done. She had burst into tears and covered her face with her hands and coughed exaggeratedly. Then she paced the room, patting her breastbone.

"No, no, no," she said, fanning her face with her hands like the heroine of a black-and-white Bollywood potboiler. "I feel terrible. Truly I do. It was *so* good I thought it was primo stuff."

And it was, thought Ullis: primo Aki.

Payal said, "Bharat, could you put the window down? I need a cigarette. I think I might be shaking a little bit."

"I thought this was a non-smoking car," said Ullis.

"But you smoke, don't you, darling?"

"Not if there's no point to it," he said, as his phone buzzed. He picked up without looking at the screen.

"I called the house and nobody answered," said his mother. Her voice was unnaturally loud in his ear. "Are you okay? Why don't you pick up when someone calls?"

"I didn't hear," said Ullis. The lie came easily. He could lie without guilt only to his mother. "I must have been in the next room, listening to music or reading or something. I might have been in the shower. Yeah, probably in the shower."

"What?"

"The shower, I was in the shower."

"What are you doing?" she asked.

"I'm at the market buying groceries. Wonderful pomegranates this time of year." Perhaps he'd gone too far, perhaps some dialling back was in order. "I mean," he said defensively, "I have to eat."

He had no idea why he didn't want his mother to know he was in Bombay. He understood, instinctively, that it was a good idea to be less than forthcoming about his whereabouts. And there was the matter of habit. He'd become so adept at hiding the truth from her that he did so automatically. Besides, she wanted to be lied to. She even expected it, particularly when it came to the big things. The least he could do was oblige. It was the duty of a dutiful son.

Beside him Payal lit a cigarette. From a small fridge hidden in the console between their seats, she retrieved a can of diet cola and a can of lager and held them out to Ullis. He pointed at the lager.

"You're a saint!" he told Payal, forgetting to cover the phone.

"It's true," said his mother. "I had to become one. But I never expected to hear you say so."

"No, no, not you. I was talking to myself."

"Oh," said his mother dejectedly. "Are you sure you're okay? Since when did you start talking to yourself?"

"There's nothing wrong with a bit of talk. I think I've always done it. It's a matter of conversing with someone I know fairly well."

"You used to walk in your sleep, did you know that?"

"Yes, I did. You've told me many times."

"Once I heard a noise and you were shutting the front door, waiting for the elevator. I don't know where you thought you were going in the middle of the night."

"I think I might have been pretending to sleepwalk. I might have been making a break for it."

"You were wearing a raincoat."

"Well, was it raining? Sometimes there's a reasonable explanation for things."

"Now, Dominic, we were thinking it might be a good idea for you to come and stay with us for a week or two. What do you think?"

He remembered the ringing quality of the silence when he got home on the night of his wife's death. He had felt it the moment he crossed the threshold: a kind of stillness, or staleness. He rushed through the rooms as the dread grew, the air already full of it, knowing what he would find and praying he was wrong. The entire hideous sequence played itself out in his head several times a day. How would he live there again? How would he go from one room to the next? Aki had installed bamboo screens on the terrace because they lived in a top-floor flat in Defence Colony that was susceptible to intense heat in the summer. She had found a man who constructed made-to-order screens backed by cool green fabric, which had transformed the terrace into a haven of shade and breeze. The screens had hardly been up for a week when she died. He hoped never to see them again.

"Well, what do you say?" his mother was asking.

He made what had become his standard reply to most, if not all questions asked of him since his wife's suicide: "I don't see why not."

"You're not back on the drink, are you? Please don't start that all over again. Appa says it is when a person's character is tested that you show the world what you are made of."

"I'm made of clay," he said, "in particular my feet and heart."

"Answer me, are you drinking again?"

"Of course I'm not drinking again," he said, which made Payal raise her eyebrows in mock, or was it genuine horror.

"Don't blame yourself," his mother said. "It's not your fault."

"It is my fault, you have no idea. Is Appa there?"

"Yes, but he doesn't want to talk right now. He'll call you tomorrow. He's taken it hard. We loved her too."

How strange it was that other people felt compelled to mourn his wife. He couldn't believe in their grief. To him it was play-acting, a simulation, people making gestures because they thought it was expected of them. In the days immediately after her death there had been phone calls from near and far. All kinds of people called, including those with whom he had lost touch. An old friend from New York had somehow managed to find his number and called at the worst time, when the last thing he wanted was to talk. When he and Aki got married, the friend had managed to convey his disapproval of the union. Ullis had no doubt that his friend's response was born out of his own loveless marriage. Soon after, he and the friend had stopped speaking. For years they didn't speak. Until, two days after Aki's death, the phone rang and Ullis unwisely answered. It was his friend, the bad news bear, on the phone from New York. Buddy, I'm sorry, he kept saying. I'm sorry, buddy. It's okay, Ullis kept replying. As always, Ullis had ended up comforting the comforter.

His former friend had followed up the call with a condolence email, a long unmemorable quote from Marcus Aurelius: "You may ask how, if souls live on, the air can accommodate them all from the beginning of time. Well, how does the earth accommodate all those bodies buried in it over the same eternity? Just as here on earth, once bodies have kept their residence for whatever time, their change and decomposition makes room for other bodies, so it is with souls migrated to the air. They continue for a time, then change, dissolve, and take fire as they are assumed into the generative principle of the Whole: in this way, they make room for successive residents." Under the quote, his friend had written: "I hope this is a source of some comfort to you."

It had been the source of some discomfort. The Aurelian argument rested on the premise that the soul lived on after death. What if one began with the assumption that the soul did not live on? What then? Well, then the earth was a prospect of unrelieved emptiness, of meaninglessness and woe, a vista of chance suffering alleviated only by a liberating death. The notion that the dead were successive occupants of the earth and the air – it did not condole and it did not console. Ullis failed to see how Marcus provided any comfort at all, unless you were in another country, safely detached from grief, firing off emails and phone calls when death visits someone you know, your real motive to massage a sense of relieved schadenfreude.

There had been many such calls and messages that added to the burden of the days. Certainly in his mother's case, when Aki was alive, it had been a different story entirely. Then it had seemed as if she and his mother were locked in a power struggle. His mother tried her best to dominate and Aki did her best to resist. Now that she was dead, all this had been forgotten.

"It was a hot night, summertime in Bombay. There was no rain."

"I beg your pardon?"

"The night you left the house in a raincoat. You were nine years old. Imagine if I hadn't found you."

"I was probably on my way to the airport."

"Are you sure," his mother said, "are you sure you're not drinking?"

"Let me call you back? There are people in line behind me."

"Okay," said his mother. "Will you call me back?"

"Of course I will," said Ullis sincerely.

He cut the call.

Bharat had put the windows up and the car was cool again. Ullis took a deep sip of the lager and put on his sunglasses and tried to delay the inevitable: another line of cocaine, another drink, some H, a smoke of hash. At some point he'd run out of these crucial diversionary measures, and then, what would happen then?

"When someone close to you commits suicide," said Payal, "it makes you consider killing yourself too. Or so I've heard. Do you think there's some *truth* to it?"

Today her sari was georgette or chiffon. She wore it the Gujarati way, on the wrong shoulder, from back to front. When she took a sip of her drink, the silver jewellery on her wrist produced a bright chink. There were nicotine stains on her fingers.

"It must have been *awful* to have to go through it, the kind of thing that throws your whole life upside down. I'm so sorry, darling."

"Thanks," said Ullis consolingly. "It's okay."

"No, it's not, it's horrendous!"

To his surprise, she started to cry. An elegant handkerchief appeared and she dabbed carefully at her eyes, checking to see that her mascara hadn't run.

"There, there," he heard himself saying. "Never mind."

Then, to his horror, he too was crying. He tried to be silent but a farrago of ragged breaths broke from his throat. In his confusion and shame he patted ineffectually at Payal's hand. He tried discreetly to flick the tears off his face but they kept falling. He cried his stupid tears and waited for the moment to pass. It did not.

"My first husband's twin brother died in his teens. They say he fell but my husband *always* thought he jumped. Really, he knew it, since they were identical twins and all. He said for a long time it made him feel as if he had died too, or the best part of him had died. But then it made him want to live all the more. Do you think that's true, darling?"

"I don't know," said Ullis, tears gathered at his chin like a jazzman's beard.

And it was true. He didn't know. He had no idea. Would Aki dead make him think about the dead in a different way? Would he see how close they were to the living, how intimate, how constant, how *there*? It could happen: your wife dies and it makes you want to live bigger. You saw above you her slender proximate shadow and it made you want to live your life for two people. Maybe it would happen to him at some point, who knew? It hadn't happened yet, of that he was sure. To want to live was a form of vulgarity, like strong opinions or a strident display of integrity. There was no surer sign of civilisation than the lack of all conviction. Who had said that? He couldn't remember. But it was on his daily checklist: the lack of all conviction, the lack of the will to live, the discreet taste for degradation, particularly in its narcotic applications. The wanting to die. For the first time he tried to admire Aki for what she had done. At least she'd taken a stand. She'd taken charge of her life. She hadn't waited around to see how it would all turn out. She'd gone all the way, whatever the cost to those who loved her. And as easily as that the resentment returned, displacing any trace of admiration.

He drank the last of the beer and made more lines, cracked the window to circulate a blast of warm air, looked in the fridge for another can, apologised that the car had become too warm, shut the window, found only bottled water in the fridge, and remembered that he didn't like beer in the first place.

When the time-release cocaine kicked in, a vintage reel of pictures unspooled in his head: Aki in the black dress she wore when they first met, Aki ordering fugu at a midtown restaurant, disappointed to learn the toxins had been removed, Aki unmoved by Bob Dylan, Aki bestowing one of her rare smiles, Aki commanding a dinner table with a story of perfidy among writers, Aki dancing alone in the centre of a room, Aki singing, Aki asleep.

Now, as promised, there follows a more detailed picture of that first meeting, which began with diversions into Mexico and Bob and continued weeks and months later into a kiss almost of death, a kiss that gave death the middle finger and combined pleasure and fear into a single indelible gesture.

Aki had walked into the empty university library early on a Saturday afternoon, when everybody else, he assumed, was still sleeping off a hangover. He'd been working on his second book of poems. He intended to send it to the publisher on Monday morning, about six months past the deadline. She'd buzzed from the street and he let her in. They shook hands and introduced themselves. He noticed that she wore a formal black dress and ankle boots, unusual attire for a young woman, considering the default uniform on campus was ripped jeans and sneakers. He showed her to a free table, helped her start the desktop and printer, pointed out the coffee machine and bathroom facilities. They worked comfortably together on nearby stations, walled off by corridors of books and desks, the library quiet but for their keyboards and the happy sound of hot water gurgling through the pipes.

Late in the evening, as they shut the library, he asked if she'd like to join him for dinner. She said yes without giving the question much thought. They walked two blocks to a bistro called Mexico and sat at a table in the centre of the room. They ordered steak tacos and rice.

"I'm not a huge fan of Mexican fare," she said, using a taco like a roti to scoop up beans and beef. "It's Indian food gone wrong, I always thought." Seeing the disappointment on his face, she lifted her glass and said: "But the Margaritas are terrific!"

Later that week they went to the Bob Dylan concert at Madison Square Garden (with which event and its particularities the reader has already been acquainted). As with Mexican cuisine, she was no fan but she went along out of kindness or passivity. He found he liked her understated manner and unflappability. It gave her an air of seriousness far beyond her years. As the weeks and months went by he noticed she rarely laughed and she was impossible to shock, not even with a proposal of marriage. She took some days to reply. When she did it was with a gift-wrapped postcard bearing a slogan in all capitals (which she presented to him at Grand Central Station). In four months they were 'woman and husband', as she liked to say. Two weeks shy of their fourth anniversary she was dead, killed by her own reckless hand.

There had been plenty of clues if only he had seen them. As he knew now, every signed proclamation she had asked him to make, every poem she had written, every email, every bit of written communication was her way of keeping a record for him in the future.

She knew his notoriously porous memory would likely retain none of it. The mail she sent him one morning after they'd entertained friends at their tiny studio apartment in lower Manhattan, that too had been a way of keeping a record. He was at work at the newspaper and she at home when the message arrived in his inbox. He pulled out his phone and looked at it now, three years after it had been sent. 'Your salad last night' was the subject, and this was the message:

Last night we served two friends
with two knives, three forks, and six spoons
in our 200 square foot
studio on the Lower East Side.
We pay 1,250 dollars a month;
it is half your salary, and used to be
all of mine before I quit.
In the large wooden bowl, which occupies half
our dinner table,
you mixed mixed greens
with tomatoes and thin-fat
slices of parmesan, lemon and butter dressing,
and uneven bits of green apple.
We ate it with seven-grain bread
from the local bakery
where the guy hits on me
(you notice but don't say anything).
The salad was fantastic.

There had been other clues, many clues he had been too stupid to notice. Early in their life together, soon after he told her about the hepatitis C virus he carried like a birthmark, she said: "Why is it you never kiss me properly? Don't you like to kiss me?"

"I love to kiss you," he'd replied. "But I'm worried I might give you the virus."

"It's spread by blood only, not sexual contact," she said. "I looked it up, you know."

"What if I have a tiny cut on my lip?"

"I'd have to have one too, and the two cuts would have to meet, and the probability of that happening is so small it's positively freakish. Seriously, I'll take my chances," she said. "You can't live in fear your whole life, Dommie. You might as well be dead."

Then she'd grabbed his face and kissed him deep, smiling all the while, enjoying his predicament. He noticed that her slender middle fingers were raised against Old Father Death.

A melody came into his head, a guitar hook, no more than two or three notes but the kind of tune that embedded itself in your skin and stayed all day and half the night. What was the song? By a band with a punk name, though the music wasn't punk, more post-grunge pop to give it a genre, the singer in a short dress and boots, her surname shared with the hippie killer who carved a swastika into his forehead. What was her name? What was the killer's name? There was a time it would have tripped off his tongue. Now he could not recall it for the life of him. Meow, he thought, I owe you a vote of thanks.

And then the band's name came to him, *Garbage*, and the words of the song popped into his head, unasked, disastrous, complete: don't believe in fear, or faith, or anything you cannot break.

He sang the verse in his head but when he got to the chorus he sang it aloud, guitar hook included, in the direction of the backpack. He hoped his lost wife would hear:

Stupid girl, stupid girl, you had everything and you wasted it.

CHAPTER NINE

Stretched on easeful white linen, Dominic Ullis considered the ceiling. The sight of ornate red tiles and airbrushed wooden cornices gave the room a sense of continuity, the sense of a tranquil domestic setting impervious to tragedy, an *abode*. He'd taken a close look at the bed sheets and assessed that the thread count was in the range of four hundred or so. It was the first comfortable accommodation he had encountered in days. His opinion of Payal rose by several appreciative notches.

They arrived as the sun began to set, spectacularly, over the coconut palms and casuarinas. As the sky turned candy pink, the Range Rover pulled into the gravelled driveway of a glass-and-brick house not far from the beach. A small retinue of staff emerged shyly to welcome them. Smiling namastes were extended, and garlands of jasmine, and honeyed welcome drinks. The grounds extended as far as Ullis could see. There was an outdoor machan with mosquito netting over the open front entrance and beds scattered around a hearth. There was a pool. There were houses and outhouses. There were two German Shepherds who came bounding out to greet their mistress and took up positions on either side of her. Payal told the cook to put the food away and issued instructions for the evening – only white flowers, tall white candles rather than electric lights, hurricane lamps on the steps leading to the front door, no music, the dining table placed on the back lawns under the mango trees – then she air-kissed Ullis and retired to her rooms upstairs, shadowed by the big silent dogs.

A man in a white mandarin-collar jacket showed barefoot Ullis to a guest room. From the large picture window he had a view of a curved wall of red brick set with irregular openings. There was an enclosed area beyond, just visible through chintz curtains. The curve of wall enclosed an emerald lawn on which a coffee table and two wooden chairs were placed. Croquet balls and a mallet lay beside folded beach chairs. It was a nice view and it was too much stimulation. What he needed was a room with no distractions except the essential. Carefully he pulled the curtains and dropped his jacket to the floor and stretched out on the bed. He'd studied the ceiling tiles and cornices and the thread count of the bed sheets. Then he got to work.

First, a pit-stop at the facilities. In the reflective cave of black granite and stainless steel that served as the bathroom, he took off his clothes and looked at himself in the mirror. The razor scars on his arms, carved in the days of rehab when pain was a kind of pleasure, the zig-zag lightning bolts and double crosses, had healed and faded. Even in his insanity (and what was rehab but a kind of insanity?) he had deployed a shred of caution. The scars were on the underside of his forearm and largely invisible even in a T-shirt. But what could be done about his face? Here was a different battlefield entirely, an advertisement against the perils of grief-stricken drug taking, and a powerful public service message: *Just don't*. There was no denying he looked badly used, if not terminally ill. The black circles under his eyes were ingrained, rubbed into the skin. The gaunt eye sockets and pinprick pupils frightening in any light. Face bloodless, lips chapped. Even his ribcage appeared more prominent than it had been a few days earlier.

All in all he was the picture of exhausted hope. How long had it been since he'd embarked on this Bombay road movie, this lost weekend that might stretch into a lost life? And was it lost really? Wasn't it more of a found weekend? Examining his eyes up close, he was astonished to discover they held a measure of innocence still. More than a measure, innocence and exhaustion represented equally. Would he ever sleep and wake naturally again, or eat with an appetite, or catch his reflection without a violent heave of loathing? But now was not the time for self-criticism in the admirable tradition of the Chinese Red Army. Now was the time for repair and reflection.

He stepped into the shower cubicle and stood under a torrent of water so scalding he had to prop his hands against the wall for support. Using the packaged toothbrush near the sink, he brushed his teeth. Using the packaged razor, he shaved the stubble off his face. Finally, the fluffy towels folded welcomingly on a granite shelf were put to gentle use by our star-crossed protagonist, Dominic Ullis.

Wrapped in a bathrobe, he went to the couch and emptied the contents of his jacket and trouser pockets on the coffee table. From the rubble of boarding pass, vial and baggie, debit and credit cards, iPod, phone and charger, ballpoint and keys, and a creased passport photo of Aki as a child of nine or ten (already serious, already beyond laughter and silliness), he extracted a hundred-rupee note, which he rolled tightly and set aside. From the backpack he retrieved Aki's ashes, and spilled some of the coarse uneven powder on the coffee table. He chopped a handsome line and removed the plastic top from the vial of heroin and chopped two more, one so thin it was a mere suggestion of a line, the other more substantial. He picked up the rolled note and saluted the photo of Aki and snorted the thin line of heroin first. Then he waited with his eyes closed and his fingers in his ears.

The rush came to him in its entirety, an electrical current that laid him flat on a beam of white light, everything forming, everything reforming, a vein of mercury that dripped slowly from the base of his skull through his ears into his calves, touching each chakra on the subtle cord from the third eye to the root.

Danny had come through at last. Heroically he had delivered the real unadulterated thing. Clean gear. A chorus rose unbidden, scrambled from Ullis's rejuvenated cortex:

Oh Danny Boy, the voices all are calling,
When I am dead as dead I well may be,
I'll be here in sunshine and in shadow,
Oh kneel and say an Ave there for me.

After a moment of prayerful nodding, he snorted the fatter line and fell back against the couch with a moan. He began the slow-motion droop into the nod, but stopped himself and snorted the line of Aki and heard the mercury drips and spinal whispers, the painless realignment of vital chakras. As the rush gathered itself into a hammer, he made a last line of heroin and went quickly to the bed and slipped between clean white sheets. In minutes the great god of nod returned – from the prairies with his feet on fire – and Ullis was dreaming awake. Misremembered phrases megaphoned his head, followed by an identity parade of characters, real and made up, living and dead, and shards of dislodged memory from the near past. Ce naiba faci, said a woman's voice in Romanian, or was it Rajasthani? Another sang a Gujarati garba. Though the words were inaudible, the melody was achingly, disastrously familiar.

"Poor Dom," he muttered, eyes moving spasmodically under closed lids. "Poor Dom."

He was driving Aki to work, an endless succession of false starts through the aggrieved streets of Delhi. His job description at the time included 'house-husband' and 'chauffeur'. In between these duties he worked on a novel, his first venture outside the enclosed and protected world of the poem. There was some freelance copy-writing and art reviewing but it was so infrequent he could hardly call it work. She was the one with the real job. Five days a week she went to an office in Connaught Place where she headed a publishing house, a dream gig that was about to end because they'd hired a supervisor, someone older to whom she would have to report. The change in circumstances had affected her personality, in particular her sleep patterns and moods. There was an increased use of red wine and a new sense of absence and distractedness. She was prone to long silences, who had always been voluble, who had blurted her thoughts as they occurred. In the car she finally said what was on her mind, enumerating each grievance like a poison dart. She felt pressured because her job was their only steady income. If not for the fact that she was the earning member she would have quit much earlier. She knew he had supported them in New York when he was working and she was not, but that felt like a long time ago and now it was all her all the time. She was trapped. She was without options. On she went in this vein, as relentless as the grind and honk of traffic, until Ullis said, stop it, stop it, do you want me to crash?

"Go on, if you're so brave," she'd said calmly, "crash the car."

And then she grabbed the wheel and pointed them towards one of Delhi's notorious Blueline buses, also known as murder buses by the frightened pedestrians who tried, sometimes successfully, to dodge them. He had managed to brake in time. They were nudged in the back by a battered Ambassador taxi, but they got away with a melon-shaped dent in the boot and nothing more. They were alive.

Communication loves concealment. Speech leaves the mouth as a set of known concealments. It falls upon the ear with a set of unknown ones. Between the dead and the living, between wife and husband, a blue lens opens like the earth seen from space. For the one who leaves, the earth and its inhabitants are unreal though inviolable. For the one who remains, there are no clear demarcations. Nothing is visible. Nothing is resolved. The old habits of concealment continue as if life and death are contiguous states.

Satisfactorily nauseous, he opens his eyes on a bed in a guest room in Alibag. Danny, you're a good man, he says on his way to the bathroom where he vomits cleanly into the Japanese-made toilet. It has always been his favourite thing about the heroin vomit, how painless it is compared to the long-drawn torture of the alcohol vomit. How easy, how pleasurable, to empty yourself, to rise, rinse and repeat. Back in the bed, he mutters to himself as the nod takes him again.

"I'm the phool fool who brought you flowers when you didn't want them. Your contempt for the poor rose . . ."

Languages mix in his head as they do when he tries to speak anything other than English. He will set out to say something in Hindi and deliver something in French. Instead of saying nasha, he'll say ganache. Instead of dheeré, ivre. And in reverse, je suis un bateau dheeré.

Aloud he says: "What we have here, ladies and gentlemen, is a rummy and a dummy."

But this is not the word he hears, borne to him from somewhere above his head in his dead wife's unmistakable timbre.

"Dommie," she says, soft and very clear.

He looks up and sees a face embedded in a corner of the ceiling. It is white as plaster, carved and gilded like the cornice. The eyes are shut, the cherub cheeks white and bloated. Her lips are moving but there is a time lag.

"Do you have any idea how awful it is to be on a plane sat next to your husband and he looks at you and says, where's my wife? What have you done with her? Can you imagine what that feels like?"

The last time they flew together was the long flight from New York to New Delhi. He'd taken his usual twenty or forty milligrams of Ambien as well as half a bottle of wine. At some point in the night he had turned to Aki and hadn't been able to recognise her. He thought it was something to do with the overhead reading light and he switched it off. But the young woman beside him remained a stranger. She was *not* his wife, was nothing like his wife. Her cold eyes, set in a pinched, unfriendly face, were judging him. It was plain to see. He interrogated her at length, asking questions only Aki would know the answers to, and that was when he understood that he was experiencing an Ambien-induced hallucination. It terrified them both.

"Is that you?"

"That's exactly what you said."

"I mean is that you there on the ceiling?"

"Yes, yes, only I am returned to tell thee," says his wife allusively.

His eyelids are dead weights, impossible to hold up. But his ears, oh, his ears hear everything, every unspoken thought and word, and his senses are newly immaculate, heightened to super-human extremes. The click of weaver ants building a nest in the green leaves outside the window, sharp in his ears. Each birdcall amplified, the peaks and valleys compressed so the softest notes gain volume. And when he opens his eyes there is his wife, in the white moulding of the cornice. He is in the presence of a fully realised apparition. It will have to be humoured.

"Is this you, foreign returned?"

"In a manner of speaking, yes, returned from hell for a last look around."

"From where in hell? Round Two of the Seventh Circle, the suicide trees of the suicide wood, the last round before the mad drop into Circles Eight and Nine?"

"There are no circles. You'll see. But first, do you have any idea how awful it is when your husband looks you in the eyes and says: Who are you? What have you done with my wife? I want her back. Stewardess, my wife is missing. She's been abducted. Do you remember?"

He remembers, of course he does. He will never forget. The New York–New Delhi flight: they were to return to India and make a new beginning. There had been a trick of the light and momentarily he had lost her. He knows now what it was: a rehearsal.

"I thought you'd been forsaken. I mean, taken."

"You kept saying the same thing. Where's Aki? It crushed me, to be looked at and not seen. By my own husband."

Her voice rings splendidly through the room, from the ceiling to every sparkling corner. It fills the emptiness with bounce.

"How poignant your spangled version of events," he says. "I would almost question my own recollection, except I was there. I remember it was night. Everybody was asleep. There was engine noise and turbulence. I was frightened when I couldn't find you. Then I realised I was hallucinating. It only lasted a few minutes."

"You were there and you were not there."

"Exactly the question I'm asking myself. Are you here or not here?"

"I'm here. You're the one who's all over the place. But I've heard this happens to the unreliable narrator."

"I'm not unreliable, you are," he says childishly, in what he hopes will be a devastating turn of phrase. It is not.

"I'm dead," she says, "which makes me more reliable than I've ever been. Can I ask you something?"

"I don't see why not."

"Have you never seen it floating out there in the open? The shape you'll take when you're dead?"

It doesn't strike him that he is litigating a ghost. The fact of her death makes no difference to the complex rush of persecution and guilt that runs like a current between them. He sees nothing, floating or stationary. There is no movement but the quotidian. How does it matter what shape he will take?

"All righty," he says, "can you do me a favour?"

"I can hardly wait. You're about to ask something unreasonable of a recently deceased woman, aren't you?"

"Can you make the brown go away?" Unwisely, he has opened his eyes. "Everywhere I look I see brown, Pantone brown . . . the exact shade of Bombay."

He gets up and lies naked on the carpet at the foot of the bed. From here he can see her better, the bloated pale face, only the lips moving, the bloated eyes half shut. She is back from hell or wherever it was that suicides went. What is she doing here? It takes great effort to open his eyes and it takes great effort to speak.

131

"Tell me why, please. Why did you do it?"

"I've been trying to tell you. I made a mistake. I called you and I heard a girl laughing in the background. I thought: I'll show him. I'm his wife. I have my rights. I knew you'd forgive me at some point, if only from weariness. Isn't it hard work, carrying so much grievance around?"

"You *were* my wife," he says, the words emerging under great strain. He isn't certain he's speaking at all. "You abdicated."

"I'm still your wife. I may be dead but we never got a divorce, in case I need to remind you."

"Until death do us part," he says. "That's as far as it extends. You gave up all farther, uh, further rights that night."

"Always your problem, Dommie, too much faith in any old thing the Church tells you. Until death do us part! Oh, please. As if death is Church-ordained, like a catechism. As if death is the end. It isn't anything really, except a slight adjustment of the consciousness, like heroin, which is why you are able to understand me and I can speak to you. Junkies are half in love with it anyway. Heroin dreams are an early taste of dying."

"I can't," he explains incoherently.

"Do you remember what you told me when I shared my dreams with you? You said I should never tell my dreams to anyone. As if I had a choice! I had to tell you. Who else could I tell? I still dream, do you know that? I still dream and now I tell nobody."

Communication *is* concealment. Tell your dreams only to those you trust, this is what he'd said. Yet she had understood it as something quite different. Or was it in the way he'd put it? He knows now the shape he will take when he is dead, the shape that floats ahead of him at all times – a gravid knot of atmospheric density caused by the words he has spoken and the missed intentions behind them.

"I want to forgive you," he says, finding his voice. "Wanting to forgive you is the worst thing that ever happened to me."

It feels like a weight has lifted from his chest at last. To have said it is enough.

"I have a bit of information for you, if you want me to be on my way that is."

"Let's hear it."

"If you want me to leave and leave you in peace, let me go. Put my ashes into fast water and let go."

"How will it help us? How will it help me?"

"Well, what do *you* think? And one more thing."

He hears a knock. He opens his heavy eyes and looks up at the ceiling where his wife's face is moulded by white plaster. Her eyes too are heavy, it seems, embedded above him like moist, lashed, salt-encrusted stars. The knock sounds again, louder now.

"Do you know the saying, he who saves one life saves the world entire?" says his wife.

"The Talmud, or the Koran," he says. "But the opposite is also true. He who fails to save one life fails to save the world."

"You should stop beating yourself, berating yourself. No one will be saved. But you already know these things."

"I doubt if I know anything. All I've accumulated is ignorance."

"You know the dead are buried or burned. We are mourned as you mourn. But then we're forgotten and you go back to your feasting. It's a form of vengeance. You *will* forget me."

"I wish."

"Or you'll try to forget."

"I will give it my best shot."

"You probably won't," she says, smiling sweetly. "'Kay then, you better go. Go home to Delhi. You can't stay away for ever. And anyway, wherever you go there I'll be."

The absolute truth of the observation strikes him, even in the midst of a heroin hallucination.

"Yeah," he says. "You're right."

"I'll see you then."

"When?"

"You better answer the door."

"Wait," he says. "When will I see you?"

"If you want me, take more heroin."

CHAPTER TEN

In his caved-in mourning suit, Ullis accepted the pair of rubber
slippers presented by the white-clad bearer. He was led through
hallways papered with chocolate-and-pink stripes to a room
where the walls were crowded with art, mostly hunting minia-
tures and watercolours that evoked a baffled nostalgia for the
British Raj. Among a scattering of oils and acrylics, he thought
he recognised Rekha Rodwittiya's totemic female warriors and
the tortured Christ of F. N. Souza. There were thin-legged
pink-gold armchairs and coffee tables piled high with books
of photography and architecture. There was a shelf of vintage
rotary phones, the black handsets polished to a high gleam. In
the corner, a fireplace in which no fire had ever been lit. On the
mantelpiece, framed photos of a glamorous couple together and
alone. The man wore a tuxedo, his bowtie undone, his full head
of hair parted in the middle. He was grinning at someone out
of the frame. The woman wore a silk sari and pearls and looked
into the camera with a tentative full-lipped smile. Ullis asked
the bearer if he knew who the couple was. Of course, said the
man: Payal Madam's parents, Master Raj and Lula Madam. The
air conditioner was on full but a sea tang hung in the air, humid
and insistent. He heard crickets and conversation and it stopped
him for a moment. It was late in the evening. The stars hung low
in the sky. How long had he been out?

Payal got up when he stumbled into view. She'd changed into a kaftan and matching turban that continued the house colour scheme of chocolate and pink. Heavy silver jewellery chinked as she kissed him. He caught an opium savour of heady spices, plum and clove and pepper.

"There you are, darling," she said, noting his freshly shaved cheeks, "rested and refreshed, I hope?"

"Anything but," he replied enigmatically.

"Anything but," she said. "Oh dear, do you mean there's simply *no* rest for the wicked?" She seemed enchanted by the idea. Smiling, she examined his face from different angles and nodded, as if pleased with the effort he had made.

He said, "But that isn't what I meant at all. Actually there's no rest for the innocent."

"Do you really think so," Payal said, her silver smile replaced by a look of concern. "I'm sure you're right."

"The wicked get plenty of rest. They sleep like babies. Nothing ever bothers them."

"No," said Payal. "Of course not. You're irrefutably correct." She placed a firm hand on his elbow. "Now come along, dear boy, I want you to meet *everyone*."

She took him to a seat at the head of the table and introduced him to the man and woman on either side, whose names he forgot as soon as he heard them. He was still resonating from being endorsed as a dear boy, a phrase he had not heard since college.

"Meet my dear friend, Ulysses, who has come a long way to join us tonight," Payal said with a flourish of the hands, as if she were presenting a Homeric hero rather than a shoeless grief-struck stranger half out of his mind on Chinese heroin and the ashes of his own dead wife.

He tripped discreetly and took a seat. Paper lanterns hung from the trees. Around the diners, who numbered no more than half a dozen, hovered at least a dozen bearers. Someone asked what he would like to drink. A glass of red wine, he said, and when the man brought it Ullis asked if he would be kind enough to leave the bottle. The woman to his left nodded angularly, candlelight glinting on a studded bindi worn high on her forehead. She had bitten fingernails and a prominent gold tooth.

"Good idea," she said. "Why be separated from the source?"

She moved closer to the candlelight so Ullis would notice the important things: that her bindi was made of Swarovski crystals, that her nose pin was a charming arrangement of interlocking stainless steel hearts, and that the skin on her face was flawlessly unlined.

"Yes," said Ullis. "I thought I'd save him some running around."

"That's extremely thoughtful of you," said the woman. "Thoughtful towards the servants and towards us also."

"What she means is, some of us aren't quite that thoughtful," said the man to his right, whose moustaches rose to the sky like a two-pronged trident. "Which reminds me of something rather amusing."

"One second," said the woman shortly. "I'm sorry, I didn't catch your name."

"Ullis," he said. "And you?"

"I'm Petronella Raj Singh," she said, "and this is Obi," indicating the man with the moustaches, who did not seem to rate a second or third name. "Come on, drink up!" She downed her whisky and held up the glass for a refill. "We must drink until we're tipsy, that's the rule. Do you think we'll have speeches tonight? I love drunk speeches."

Ullis settled himself more securely in his chair. He put his feet squarely on the ground and placed his hands on the table. He reminded himself to be alert to tremors, the early rumblings below ground. For signs and portents he kept an eye on the lanterns among the trees. He was looking for the telltale waver, the bounce of air.

"Uma Sinh drives a Mercedes E-class coupé, as you know, a low-slung automobile quite inappropriate for Indian roads. Each dent costs about fifty thousand to repair, something I discovered much later," Obi was saying to the table. "Well, she received a place by the lake at Kamshet as part of her dowry and we're driving there, just rolling along, when she tells us to get out of the car and walk. She was absolutely serious. So the driver, the major-domo and me, we get out and trot alongside the car like bloody Kim Jong-un's bodyguards. And in the driver's seat is Uma Sinh, carefully skirting every bump and pothole."

"I'd forgotten how much you dislike her," said Petronella.

"Do I?"

"Of course you do. You said she only talks to you if she can't find someone more important. You said her eyes are always moving around the room, looking for someone richer and more famous."

Petronella had forgotten that she too disliked Uma. Why, though? For one thing, the woman had never dyed her hair. Like Payal, she wore grey hair as if she were making a holier-than-thou fashion statement. Unlike Payal, she had never invited Petronella home. At the moment, Petronella's hair was an electric shade of deep crimson. She was a Page Three fixture, which meant she had certain obligations. The photographers were crazy for a bit of colour. It was one of her duties, providing colour for the camera. Another was to take care of herself. She gnawed ineffectually at her bitten-down nails and assessed her still empty tumbler of whisky and came to a decision: she would switch to red wine. Permanently. She had become a femme d'un certain âge and she needed all the resveratrol she could get.

"I can't imagine a few dents on her Mercedes would lead Uma to bankruptcy," Petronella said.

"Oh, I am not so sure of that," said a woman with a cigarette holder held between her thumb and forefinger, like a gold-nibbed dart. "A family fortune is not limitless, especially if you are a woman and you haven't beefed up the bloodline." She looked around for support. "Wouldn't you say so?"

"I trust that barb wasn't aimed at me?" said Payal from the other end of the table. "Brinda darling, let me hasten to remind you that I have a son who's just completed his master's and is coming along absolutely swimmingly, *thank* you very much."

"Um," said Brinda darling, shrugging exaggeratedly. She was screwing a cigarette into the holder with evident enjoyment. It was Uma she'd been thinking of, but anything that rattled Payal was a plus.

"In any case," Obi continued, "it was a long and tiresome journey. I've never had so much exercise in my life. And it really is my least favourite thing in the world, you know. Exercise. We kept jumping out of the blasted car and running alongside and then jumping back in. She only let us in depending on how good or bad the road was. There was a hierarchy to the way she did it too. I was first, then the driver, and last and least was the bearer, the major-domo, who was let in only at the end and reluctantly at that. He was an old man, pretty frail and quite easily winded, I thought."

"Oh snap, that's our Uma all over," said Petronella. "She's actually *amazing*. She was the first woman in India to get a boob job. Did you know? This was in the eighties."

There was silence, but only for a moment.

"I worried the major-domo was going to have a heart attack," said Obi, refusing to be interrupted. He spoke with his hands, his thin expressive fingers shaking slightly. "I even told Uma to let the fella sit in the car. It will delay us horribly if he croaks, I told her, and that at least got through."

"*Did* she let him back in?" Petronella interjected. "Did she? Please say yes? I couldn't bear it otherwise."

"She did," said Obi magnanimously, "but then she made the driver trot alongside, sweating in his heavy uniform. He had to run and run until we gained the paved road. At one point, I swear I'm not making this up, at one point she tells me not to lean against the upholstery. Had some cockeyed theory that if we sat on the edge of our seats it would help elevate the car's centre of gravity, or some such. The poor driver was quite done in by the end of it. You could see he was considering a less dubious form of employment."

"Oh, bugger," said Brinda, through the cigarette holder lodged in her teeth. "Keeping servants is not worth the candle, no? But what else are we supposed to do? Keep a robot?" She pronounced it *roh-boh*, as if the word had been taken wholesale from the French. Around her, the white-clad bearers moved. If they heard, they gave no indication.

"There's no alternative, really," said Obi dejectedly, his cheeks flushed a dull red, his eyes watery. He was already drunk and he wasn't drunk enough. He was never drunk enough. The more he drank the soberer he got. It was the bane of his life, next to deadly dull dinner parties. At least Uma, for all her faults, was erstwhile royalty.

"Oh yes, there is alternative," said a man who had been silent until then, a dapper figure in white kurta-pyjamas, black moustache clipped almost to the skin, rings on all his fingers. His voice was high and serrated, as if he had shouted himself hoarse. He sounded nothing like the soft-voiced sophisticates around him. "Why not learn how to servant yourself? Is it impossible? Look at Americas. Even the rich people are their own servants, why not us?"

"This is Niranjan," said Payal to Ullis. "Everyone calls him Ninja." She provided a brief biography – politician, family man, businessman – and then she said something about the tallest statue in the world. "Without Ninja it would never happen, God forgive us."

Ullis drained his glass and felt a quick stab of nausea. He'd forgotten the old rule. Do not mix drink with heroin unless you have a nearby restroom in which to vomit. The conversation certainly wasn't helping. He couldn't understand it when people got so excited about politics. What else did they expect from their elected representatives, tenderness and conscience? It was like expecting a goose to appreciate the semantics of *boo*, or a scorpion to save his sting for a more opportune time. As long as they didn't start bashing the American president he didn't mind. At this low point in his life and in the life of the world, the president was more than necessary. He was the inadvertent truth-teller, a lodestar to the future, and, most of all, he was a comfort to the troubled mind. You knew things were bad, but at least they would get worse, as long as he was around.

"Why don't they refuse to put up with us?" said Petronella. "Why don't they overthrow us? Surely they outnumber us by millions and millions? How I wish they would do it quickly and get it over with."

The phrase delighted her. She decided to use it the following day when she was to appear on a television panel, *India: The State of the Nation.* Everything she knew about the state of the nation would fit on half her phone screen, but it was more than enough for the limited purposes of television punditry. She'd learned the important thing: it wasn't what you said, it was how you said it. She would wear her new white-and-blue Raw Mango sari, which showed well on screen, and she'd ask why the poor of India were so passive. Didn't they *want* to improve their lot? It would play perfectly on prime time. The liberals on her panel would scream themselves silly. When she grinned, the candlelight glinted roguishly on her gold tooth and crystal bindi.

"In this country there will never be the French Revolution," said Niranjan to Ullis. "Never! Okay?"

"Okay," said Ullis obediently.

"We are Hindu," said Niranjan with satisfaction, his high voice hoarse and forceful. "We know this life is full illusion. If it is too unbearable, don't mind. Next one will be better." His thick beringed fingers picked up the glass of whisky sitting by his elbow. "Plus, there is one more thing. We are Hindu but we are not elitist. Got it?"

"Got it," said Ullis.

"We know even chaiwallah can become the pee yem."

"He was never a chaiwallah," said Payal. "That's an alternative fact, darling, out and out nonsense, a barefaced po-faced quite horrid lie. Don't you know our brave leader manufactures fake news by the bucketful?"

"Payal, please mind it," said Niranjan sharply. "Let us not have spoilage of the dinner. You are welcome to enjoy your opinions but is it necessity to share them with guests? I think no."

A silence fell and lengthened across the table. It was broken by a hesitant voice with an urgent plea.

"Excuse me," said Dominic Ullis. "Could you point me in the direction of a restroom?"

"Yadav will show you," Payal said, dismissing the man with a wave of her hand. Then: "Are you all right, darling? You don't look *well*, a bit green around the gills I'd say."

He followed Yadav into the house, and hurried past the French windows and down a flight of stairs to a bedroom. Lamplight shone on a desk strewn with books and magazines. A muted television was tuned to CNN. From a large metal cage lined with newspaper a parrot stared at the screen. The ceiling fan was turned up high.

There was a hum in the room, the old life set ajar.

"African Grey," said Yadav, nodding at the parrot. "His name is Mr Paul."

Then he pointed to a door set squarely in the middle of the far wall. Ullis rushed in and lifted the toilet seat just in time to vomit into the bowl. The sight of the vomit made him feel better almost instantly. At least now he was ready for more heroin. Using a tissue to clean the top of the toilet tank, he laid out a modest line that he commandeered in a trice. He flushed twice and sat for a moment with his head in his hands.

Emerging from the bathroom, he noticed a white stain on his trouser cuff. It might have been whitewash or paint or toothpaste. Where had it come from? The size of a thumbprint, yet it seemed terribly prominent and impossible to ignore. He tried to brush it off but it wouldn't go. After a while he sat on the bed and stared at his useless hands. He stared at the strange white stain. There was a heavy feeling in his chest that would not lift. It came to him that he was trying not to cry.

Mr Paul the parrot, newly agitated, squawked at him in a language that might have been English. He seemed to be saying, "Death is off it." Or, "Death is profit." Or even, "Death, stop it." Whatever it was saying, the death-obsessed African Grey was anxious to be released from his cage. His wide-open eyes held as clear an expression of madness and intelligence as Ullis had ever seen. He stared at the parrot and the parrot stared back. A moment of understanding passed between them. The Grey grabbed the top of the cage with his great hooked beak and, hanging upside down, said in a stage whisper, "What's up? What's up?" His eyes stared unblinkingly.

"Yes," said Ullis, at a loss for words. "Not very much, I'm afraid."

"Uh oh, Django," said the bird, broadcasting from the end of the world, sharing breaking news with the planet's last denizens. "Death is toffee. You know what I mean?"

"I think I do," said Ullis, feeling better for some reason. If death was toffee, how bad could it be? Coming from a creature that had spent its life in a metal cage, his own troubles were put into perspective. He said, "Hang on and I'll have you out of there."

He found the switch for the fan and turned it off before opening the small tin door of the cage. The parrot whistled wolfishly and made no move to exit his prison.

"Go on then," said Ullis. "What are you waiting for?"

"Death is awful," said Mr Paul.

"Yes, yes, right you are," said Ullis. "A metaphysic, a credo, a doctrine for our times. There's no clear way around it, is there?" And when the African Grey didn't respond, he said, "Well, I'll leave you to it."

Outside the room he paused for a moment, swaying deliciously. The booster snort powered its way through his synapses, shutting down unnecessary systems and firing up the nightlights. He closed the door softly behind him and went up the stairs, the stain on his cuff forgotten.

They were still discussing the statue of Shivaji.

"*Don't* you think," said Payal, "there are better ways to spend five hundred million dollars? Education, for instance? The eradication of hunger? Rural health initiatives? Roads that won't, like, kill us? Monsoon preparedness? Ending power cuts? But no, we get a statue to a king who's been dead these five hundred years."

Petronella wanted to applaud. She didn't agree with Payal, not by a long shot. But she liked the way she stood up to Ninja. Nobody else had the gumption, certainly not her. There were easier battles and she preferred to pick one she might win.

"It is a great difficulty, believe me," said Niranjan. "Chinese are making 208 metres tall statue to Buddha. When they heard of our statue, which was 210 metres, they increased height by two metres."

"Bugger," said Brinda wearily. The dinner had hardly begun and already she needed a nap. What she really wanted was to go home. Using her finger, she mixed her whisky and soda. She said: "Bugger the Chinese, always trying to outdo everyone."

Do they? thought Petronella. Do they really, or is our Brinda a bit of a racist? She smiled appreciatively and realised she was enjoying herself. Even the unlikable Brinda seemed sweet and forlorn.

"Yes, yes," said Niranjan. "But this time they are extinguished at their own game. We have increased height more." He clapped his hands. "More!"

"How much?"

Niranjan cagily steepled his fingers. "Cannot disclose," he said. "Secret."

Unable to stop herself, Petronella clapped. She hoped it would endear her to Niranjan. Annoyingly, Brinda followed suit.

Deploying her golden smile, Petronella said, "Hurrah?"

Not to be outdone, Brinda waved her cigarette holder like a flag and said, "Bravo, bravissimo!"

"Yes," said Niranjan, sitting back in his chair, his hands clasped across his trim stomach. "We have increased overall height of our statue by additional metres. It will be extra ordinary marvel, wonder of the whole world. And believe you me, after it is built, all you peoples who like to kit-pit? *You* will be saying thank you for making India great!"

MAKE INDIA GREAT AGAIN, thought Ullis, imagining a designer line of red ball caps embroidered with the Om symbol, sold online for a couple of thousand rupees each. The punters of the new India would snap them up in a minute. He imagined a business plan and a pitch for venture capital. He imagined the life of a ball cap tycoon. He imagined plush accommodation and the serene knowledge that he would never again fly economy.

"Ninja darling, how terribly clever of you," said Payal witheringly, signalling to the bearers to serve the main course and replenish the guests' drinks. "And by the way, it's the tallest statue in the world only when you count the pedestal."

"Correct," said Niranjan, surprised. "You are exceedingly correct."

"Tallest in the world and undoubtedly the ghastliest," said Payal.

Ullis thought she was younger than she appeared at first glance, the silver hair offset by the youthfulness of her features. But why didn't she mention the real point about building statues in the sea, however tall or expensive or misguided? How futile it was, like writing your name on water, like building a home or office or bank and inviting the sea to make itself at home among the books, the framed photos, the electronics and furnishings. Why did no one mention this? Didn't they notice the heat and wildfires, the hurricanes and cyclones and mudslides and floods, the drought and famine, the biblical pestilence that had already begun to fester, whether you lived in Hongkong, or Florida, or Bombay? Didn't they hear the hum of disturbance?

A man in white appeared at his elbow with a sealed clay pot of biryani. Another man in white augmented the biryani with a katori of pomegranate yoghurt and removed his untouched plate of tenderloin medallions. It was Ullis's kind of dinner party, individual portions placed in front of you and taken away without comment. No awkward passing around of dishes. Just endless talk of poverty while dinner guests stuffed their faces. He replenished his glass of wine and filled the glasses of his neighbours. He pierced the skin of the dum pukht biryani with a fork and let the steam rise from the pot. Carefully he ate some of the meat and the fragrant yellow rice. Chewing was an unfamiliar sensation, as was swallowing, as was the heat the food left in its wake. He took another cautious bite, the first solid food he had had all day, if not in days, if not in his entire life. It took all his concentration to chew and swallow.

"You Englishwallahs," said Niranjan, and his rough voice put a damning emphasis on the last word, "are not representatives of

India. I think your sympathies are with British Raj, not Swaraj. This is why you hate yourselves. Is it not so?"

"Ninja, at least the British gave us one or two things that have endured," said Payal. "What has *your* lot given us except fear and hatred and lynchings on the street in broad daylight? How medieval we have become all thanks to you!"

"You are a rich woman," said Niranjan, gesturing at a bearer to refill his whisky glass.

"Ah, ah," said Payal, "not that again."

"But it's true. You live in five-star hotel with servants everywhere, and you talk like communist, like Marxist-Leninist, like Naxalite! Is that not hypocritical?"

"I can't help where I was born," said Payal, putting down her glass with a heavy thud. "I can't help my last name or my circumstances. But I know whom to trust."

Dominic Ullis at the head of the table – there and not there, distracted, listening to one woman's voice and hearing another's – took a deep mouthful of wine that brought back the nod: the conversation receded to a blessed distance.

It was midwinter. He was on his way to Pennsylvania on assignment for the newspaper. She wore a faux fur coat and a wide hand-knitted scarf. Her sunglasses were tortoiseshell black ovals that covered half her face. She was all lips and tousled hair. She'd insisted on coming to see him off. She had nothing better to do, she said, and she was always a sucker for goodbyes. They burrowed into the deep leather armchairs near the lost and found office under Grand Central. Before he boarded the train, she gave him a gift-wrapped postcard and hugged him as if they'd never meet again. On the train he held up the card: the words *IF NOT NOW THEN WHEN?* in black capitals against a plain white background. It was her way of saying yes to his proposal of marriage made some days earlier. He had fallen asleep with the postcard on his chest, and woken with the sensation that the words had burned into his skin and burrowed inside his brain.

Unwisely, he took another sip of wine. He got up quickly and rushed down the stairs to the toilet and vomited again. Which called for another line. When he came out, he noticed he'd left the bedroom door open and Mr Paul the oracular African Grey was nowhere to be seen.

He paused at the bottom of the stairs. Tiredness had set up camp in his joints, all the tiredness in the world gathered inside his bones and skull. He counted the steps as he climbed, twelve from the bedroom up to the living room, a dozen ascending obstacles. There was no sign of the parrot anywhere. In the courtyard the guests had abandoned dinner. Payal stood by the bar smoking, deep in conversation with Petronella and Obi. It seemed that Brinda and Niranjan were preparing to leave. It was clear the argument about the tallest statue in the world had not been resolved to anyone's satisfaction.

"Time for us to go, I'm sorry to say," said Brinda, who didn't look sorry at all.

"We must go or we'll miss last speedboat," said Niranjan.

Ullis said, "Back to Bombay?"

"Yes, yes. We can give you a lift, if you'd like?"

He hesitated only for a moment. "I don't see why not," he said.

"Do come," said Brinda.

"Yes," said Ninja, after the most minuscule of pauses, "you are welcome to join. Please come."

It took him only a few minutes to take his leave of Payal, who said a driver would take them to Mandwa jetty. She told him to feel free to drop in and see her any time he pleased.

"Thank you for everything and especially for the slippers," he said, pointing at the rubber flip-flops on his feet. He was oddly reluctant to say goodbye to her.

"*Such* a pleasure, dear boy," she said, lowering her voice. "Do come and see me again. After all, we're blood brothers now, aren't we, darling? Aren't we siblings of the sibilance?" She tapped her nose meaningfully.

Brinda waved goodbye, but Niranjan did not even glance in Payal's direction as he walked smartly out of the courtyard towards the driveway. As the Range Rover set off for the jetty, a figure came running alongside. Yadav was at the window, panting gently. He handed Ullis his backpack with its precious white box.

"Thank you," he said to Yadav. "Awfully sorry to make you run."

"So thoughtful," said Brinda, echoing Petronella with a slight edge to her voice. "I can hardly believe it."

Ullis thought he saw a flash of African Grey in the trees as the car pulled away. He hoped it was Mr Paul fending for himself in the wilds of Alibag, free at last to come and go as he pleased, learning new words for the old world, learning to forget the preparations for death. For a moment his nausea lifted and he thought of his dead wife's spirit winging with delight, like a freed bird, across the orchards and into the sky.

CHAPTER ELEVEN

What does it mean to be at sea, to be off-line, untethered to the earth, bounded on all sides by deep water? You give yourself to sky that is the colour of water and water the colour of sky. You let the tide guide you to a place of odd mercy. For Dominic Ullis, the sensation of being at sea led not to confusion but to clarity – and to a funeral.

They cleared the driveway of Payal's bungalow and gained a narrow tree-lined road on which moonlight fell in leaf-shaped shards. Niranjan disliked being in Payal's SUV, driven by Payal's driver, but he would bear his animus in silence. He and his wife had left their car at home and taken a speedboat to Alibag because they did not want to go the long way round from South Bombay. He'd looked forward to an evening away from politics and politicians, a light dinner, local seafood, some whisky and conversation and a fresh sea breeze. Instead there was poached and seared this and that, soulless chef's fare served in a pit of cobras, with Payal as chief cobra, the most dangerous nagin of them all. And now they were stuck with the man in the black suit, one more self-hating Englishwallah, like all of Payal's friends – snobs and scoundrels who pretended not to know their own language and hoped never to be caught speaking Hindi or Marathi or Tamil. Westernised liberal elitists were the true enemy of the nation, on a par with Pakistanis and terrorists. He went out of his way to have no interaction with the type, but the black suit fellow had begged to come with them. What to do but bear it too? Though this would not be borne in silence.

"Payal mentioned you recently became widower," said Niranjan, comfortably splayed in the back seat. "My condolences."

It was the kind of word you never expected to hear, *widower*. It was the kind of word you never thought would apply to yourself. It reminded Ullis of a photo feature he had seen, a black-and-white magazine supplement about the widows of Varanasi, women of all ages from all over the country, their personalities obliterated by the Indian woman's bereavement uniform of white sari, no bindi, no jewellery, no colour. The dazed faces said it all, how it felt to be the defunct wife, the embodiment of regret and renunciation and the worst bad luck. What about the widowers? Did they too wear white for the rest of their lives, taking to mourning as if to a new job? They did not. They'd invented the system, old men with dying on their minds, who wanted to ensure their wives remained enslaved even after they were gone. But who was Ullis to complain about Indian funerary practices? He could hear them now: *What kind of widower is he, out and about in his black suit? Doesn't he care that the Indian colour of mourning is white? And what kind of name is Dominic Ullis? Sounds Greek to me.*

"Yaar," said Brinda tiredly, "I'm so sorry for your loss."

"Is that the Indian yaar or the American yeah?" said Niranjan unexpectedly.

Ullis kept his eyes on the road, glad to be sitting in front, grateful for the unbroken silence that ensued. He hoped it would last all the way to the waterfront and he wouldn't have to console people he did not know. He kept his eyes on the road and his feet squarely on the ground. He watched for signs and portents, tremors in the trees, a rent in the salt air. He listened for the hum of disturbance.

They passed a small market village, a collection of ramshackle storefronts and sleeping dogs and a battered red postbox. New concrete in wet squares took up most of the road and the driver had to slow the car to a crawl. They passed a sign that named the village as Chondhi. Then they were back on the road turned now into a strip of black silver in the moonlight.

"Hurry, or we'll miss it," said Brinda when the Range Rover stopped at Mandwa jetty.

She was first out of the car, walking fast in her city heels, Niranjan following, running now and then to catch up. Ullis grabbed his backpack and joined them in the long dash to the end of the pier, past speedboats and ferries and small vessels battened down for the night. The jetty, newly built by a clothing company, ran parallel to the skeleton of an older jetty whose antique concrete pilings sat stolidly in the water. In the dull light of the moon everything was shadow and pity. At the jetty's end they saw a sign, *Juggie's Marine Service*, and came to a boat that had not been built for speed. There was a bench along the back and no life preservers. A man sat on deck watching a video on his cell phone, his face white in the light of the screen. He got up to greet them as they climbed aboard one by one, careful not to lose their footing on the small buoyant vessel. Brinda, shaky on her heels, grabbed Niranjan's arm. The night was settling into the boat, seeping into its woodwork, turning its edges blood red. Ullis held firm to his only possession, the backpack.

"Thank God," Brinda said, dropping her handbag on the bench and taking off her shoes. "I thought we would surely miss the last boat. All that natak at Payal's, I'm tired. I want to go home, Ninja."

"Who doesn't?" said Niranjan.

"Me," said Ullis. "I don't, not just yet. Maybe never."

"Chalo, Captain Jagdish," Niranjan said. "Time to go."

"You call me Juggie, short for Jagdish," said the boy, pointing at the Marine Service sign.

"Okay then, Captain Juggie."

But Juggie hadn't finished with his sales pitch and the words floated off his tongue with the ease of long practice.

"Juggie stays open later than other boats your safety is my concern," he said. "Charges are lesser you can pay Juggie now or after landing by cash or GPS card machine as per your wish!"

Seventeen or eighteen at most, gym-built, wearing a muscle tee and falling-down jeans, he wasn't old enough to drive, much less take a boat into choppy waters. But his confidence was supreme. He was the new Indian, uninterested in the past, dazzled by a future indistinguishable from money. Aki and the boy captain were separated by less than a decade in age, but she might have been from a different species. She'd grown up in the same city, in an apartment in a far suburb, an only child left to her own devices. She listened to the cries and entreaties from the playground nearby, and wandered among rooms filled with her father's books, the smell of spider dust and paper in the air. The boy captain had none of her anxiety or damage or glorious doubt. His imagination circled around visions of cash money. His pride lay in his printed T-shirts and embroidered jeans, and his pastime was watching Hindi music videos on his phone. He was happy. He and Aki had nothing in common.

The small boat rocked as Ullis took a seat, and his thoughts returned to the afternoon he first met Aki's father.

It was the summer of the year they moved back to India. Aki

hadn't seen her father since leaving the country at the age of eighteen. Her father had never met her husband. When they got married, she'd mailed photos of the wedding at City Hall. In return he'd sent a rambling letter with his thoughts on marriage and a photocopy of an article he'd published on the subject. Written in Marathi, in his unreadable hand, Aki had had to decipher and translate line by line. Her father wrote that he did not allow himself to be swayed by the common conviction that marriage occurred only once in a person's lifetime. In fact, it was his theory that it was necessary to marry again and again until one got it right. As Aki read the letter out in English, she laughed. It was provocation, something her father liked to do in his articles. He meant no harm, Ullis would see.

They flew to Bombay and took a taxi to the suburb in which he lived, an old mixed neighbourhood of residential buildings and office blocks that Ullis had never visited. It was a Saturday afternoon, hot and very quiet. They walked down empty streets where plane trees dropped bristly seed balls on wide sidewalks and shaded low-rise buildings. There was no traffic. The parks were empty. Even the dogs had gone away. It was as if they were the only people left alive in the world.

They came to a small Hanuman temple, the front pillars covered with brass bells, uvulas slack like knotted tongues. Turned translucent by sun and rain, the bells had acquired the colour of unglazed pottery. There were hundreds of them, placed around the pillars in orderly rings. The ceiling and portico supported bigger bells that hung from blood-red iron beams. Near the inner shrine great metal maces stood bunched like giant vegetables. And in the innermost space tiny finger bells were arrayed across every surface.

Aki said each bell was an expression of gratitude by someone whose prayers had come true. On Tuesdays and Saturdays they rang for hours, building to a crescendo heard throughout the neighbourhood. She'd loved the sound as a child. When she was sent away to live with relatives, she would listen for the bells and sometimes she would almost hear them. Even now she missed it. Even now she associated the pealing of the bells with the happiest time of her life.

She took him in through the gates and they each rang a bell in their bare feet and they each made a wish. Later, holding hands, they walked through the old neighbourhood towards her father's house, the streets unexpectedly quiet and lovely for a far Bombay suburb. How were they to know that those wishes made in the hope of happiness would turn to ashes in less than three years? In time to come, he would be convinced that it was the making of the wish that had crushed theirs into a small white box. The bells had turned against them.

Aki's father was then in his seventies, a shirtless man wearing a pair of pale cotton bell-bottoms rolled to his knees. Ullis noted his hairless bony chest and extreme thinness as he let them into an apartment dominated by a large front room, the room dominated in turn by two desks in the shape of an L, surrounded on all sides by piles of newspapers and books. On the wall behind his chair were phone numbers and names scrawled thickly in pencil, and doodles and reminders in Marathi, some of the markings crossed out and written over. Her father had asked no questions about their journey to Bombay or their life in New York. He had shown no curiosity about the daughter he hadn't seen in six years. All he wanted to talk about was his life, his work, his day.

"This is where I sit," he said to Ullis, pointing to the cluttered desks. "I am freelance journalist in Hindi and Marathi, daily columnist for *Dainik Bhaskar*. Have you met Colin Wilson?"

Startled, Ullis said that he had not.

"Then you must meet him," said Aki's father. He picked up a well-used copy of a book by the writer and flipped through so Ullis would see the copious annotations he had made in Marathi. "I meet him regularly."

Ullis, looking around for Aki, said, "I once read his attacks on H. P. Lovecraft and Aleister Crowley. I think he called them biographies."

"Yes!" said Aki's father. "Yes! Do you have them? Please send to this address."

And he presented Ullis with a card and said something in Marathi to Aki. Blank-faced, she paid no attention. She was walking around the room she had known as a small child, picking things up and putting them down. She examined a battered photo album and a pressure cooker placed on a waist-high pile of old newspapers. As Ullis accepted the card, his father-in-law launched into a lecture on Colin Wilson's 'most brilliant' *The Outsider*. His main point was the book's continuing relevance to 'modern questions of existence and nothingness'.

From across the room Aki said, "What modern question of existence? What modern nothingness? Nobody I know cares about that stuff. Existentialism is so twentieth century."

She was looking at a calendar that had all twelve months arranged across a single page. It was September but her father's scribbles extended to December and beyond.

"I am writing series of articles on Colin Wilson for *Dainik Bhaskar*," said her father, as if she hadn't spoken. "Colin Wilson is extraordinary writer. Can you guess how many books?"

"Sorry?"

"How many books Colin Wilson has written?"

Ullis became aware that a young woman had entered the room from the kitchen. She carried a tray with a teapot and mugs.

"I couldn't imagine," said Ullis.

"Guess," said his father-in-law. "Don't be scared. Just guess!"

"Fifteen?" said Ullis, aiming for as large a number as possible. "Twenty-five?"

There was a manic, hysterical sound: his father-in-law was laughing. Ullis noticed that the old man had no teeth, and it struck him that he'd seen a pair of dentures in a saucer on a stack of *National Geographic* magazines. The girl who had entered stayed where she was at the far end of the room, still holding the tray.

"More than hundred. Colin Wilson wrote more than hundred books," he said. "Have tea. Have tea. Kamala, three cups!"

The girl put down the tray and wiped her hands on her salvaar. Her red nail polish was chipped and bright against her dark skin. Self-consciously she smoothed the straightened hair that fell stiffly to her plump shoulders.

Aki returned from her perambulations around the room with a book that had broken into pieces. She held the slabs carelessly in her hands. The front cover was adorned with fountain pen markings in her father's tight, illegible scrawl. There was some comfort in this. It reminded her of the books of her childhood, the covers marked by his fountain pen, the pages dog-eared, marginalia spilling into the text.

"I want this," she told him unhappily, holding up the book. Her eyes were on the girl pouring tea into three mugs.

"This is Kamala," said her father. "She is living with me. Her parents requested me to help."

Kamala, dark and round-cheeked, was no more than twenty-one or twenty-two, younger than Aki by several years. She smiled shyly but the smile faltered and faded.

"I'm from Baroda," she said, and took a step back towards the kitchen as she became aware of Aki's unsmiling scrutiny.

There was a short exchange in Marathi between Aki and her father. He took the book from her hand and examined it as if for the last time. He brushed with his thumb the ornate lettering of the title *The Art of Loving* and the graphic, a pink heart shape that enclosed a bouquet of flowers, and then his thumb traced his own inky rounded scrawl that trailed across the title and the cover image. With a flourish he presented the book to his daughter.

"When she came to me," he said to Ullis, who was unsure whether the old man was referring to Aki or Kamala, "she had very bad odour, very offensive. I made her change her diet. Now she smells much better. Is it not so, Kamala?"

Kamala said nothing, but there was defiance in her silence and her poise. She lifted her head and pushed her straightened hair behind her ears. Her gaze went blank when it rested briefly on the old man. Oblivious, he slurped his tea and gasped in pleasure.

Aki and Ullis exchanged a look and imperceptibly she shook her head: *I wish we hadn't come. I want to get out of here.* From the playground came the cries of schoolchildren. Somewhere a motorcycle backfired. Only the old man felt no awkwardness in the silence that followed. He was scribbling on an article in an issue of *The Economist*. As if continuing a conversation with himself, he said: "I have told her I will leave this house to her if she looks after me when I am old, I mean older." The high-pitched laugh exploded into the room and was abruptly cut off.

159

Kamala put a bowl of sugar on the L-shaped pair of desks. She arranged her hair behind her ears and smoothed her salvaar and gathered herself up with dignity. When she spoke, it was to Aki: "I told him I don't want anything. I only want to continue my studies. I want to join college, maybe in UK."

At this she and the old man exchanged a few rapid words in Marathi. It sounded like an ongoing argument about the advisability or not of going abroad for higher studies.

When Aki and Ullis finished the tea, they took their leave of her father. He waved without looking up from his work. The girl had disappeared into the kitchen. As they retraced their steps to the main road and the wide sidewalk scattered with seed balls, Aki examined the book she had taken from him. It had come apart again and she was trying to put the pieces together in the correct sequence.

"The house should be my inheritance. Instead he's giving it away to that girl," she said, her voice low and unnaturally steady. "This book is all he left me and even that he didn't give willingly."

They found a taxi, the driver asleep in the back with his feet in the window. Dusk was falling and the streetlights came on. As they got into the car the bells began to toll.

Jagdish slipped the jetty rope and gunned the engines. They made a slow turn around the pier in a quick pull of ascending noise. Behind them, Alibag dimmed into violet light. The little boat skimmed the waves and the spray hit them full in the face. The moon hung before them, marking a white staircase on the sea, narrow wavering steps that led nowhere. Nobody spoke, but held tight to the handrails and the boat chugged into deep water. There was light enough to know that the water was clean and fast moving, and this was when Dominic Ullis had his epiphany. In his head, phrases repeated like a tune heard in infancy and never forgotten.

"Juggie, please," he said. "Could you stop the boat for a few minutes?"

"But why?" said Brinda. "We're in the middle exactly of nowhere."

"I'm sorry, I'm sorry, it's just that this . . . I don't know where else to find clean water in Bombay, not to mention the whole of India. I might not get another chance."

"But what are you saying?" said Brinda.

"I want to disperse my wife's ashes. Immerse, I mean. I want to immerse them," said Ullis. "Here, I promise."

What was he promising? He didn't know.

"You want to immerse your wife's ashes," said Niranjan. "Here?"

"It will only take a minute," Ullis said. "I promise."

A quick look passed between Brinda and Niranjan of incredulity or irritation. With no warning at all, a dinner party that had begun with an ideological attack by the hostess had unravelled into a funeral rite. What could be done about it? Absolutely nothing, that much was clear. Brinda shrugged as graciously as possible and nodded at Niranjan to take charge.

He said, "Then what we are waiting for, captain baba? Stop the boat!" And exactly as if he had heard the words playing in Ullis's head, he clapped him on the back and said: "Now is the time."

The sudden absence of engine noise. The boat rocking in the violet. The smell of seaweed and diesel. In the deep silence that followed, broken only by the slap of the waves, Dominic Ullis

161

took a box out of his backpack and rubbed at his eyes. He looked in his pockets for a baggie of some sort and found Danny Blow's card, creased now and dusted with pocket lint. He scooped some of the ashes into the card and folded it and put it away. Then he buttoned his jacket and shot his cuffs. The boat moved on a swell. He stepped to the handrails and gently upturned the box, emptying the contents over the side. For a moment the ashes sat on the water like a pile of small feathers. Then they turned white and solid and curved into the sea, a school of pale fish or a flock of seagulls. He could not tell if they had dissolved entirely or if it was a trick of the moonlight that some traces lingered still, cleaving to the boat.

He gripped the rails and stared into the water, the amniotic fluid from which she had come and into which she had returned. How easy it would be to slip in and let go and sink, to breathe inside the deep. Nobody would attempt a rescue, certainly not the politician or his wife and not the boy with the new jeans. How easy to fall and drift to the bottom like a heavy sundered leaf.

He noticed they were all standing, Brinda and Niranjan and he. Even Jagdish stood with folded hands, head solemnly bowed. When had the boat ride become a church service?

"Do you want to say something?" asked Brinda.

"Somebody should, no?" said Niranjan.

"I can't," said Brinda, "I have limited experience of grief only."

"I can do, but is not my place," said Niranjan. He gestured at the sea, then at the sky, and finally at Ullis.

"You do it, sir," said Jagdish to Ullis. "If anybody should say few words it is you, isn't it?"

"Yes," said Ullis, unable to continue.

Niranjan nodded briskly. He had begun to warm to the widower.

After all, he was not a bad fellow, even if he did not have Marathi. He had an honest face. And at least he was determined to follow the correct Hindu practice regarding his dead wife.

"This is good water body," Niranjan said, his voice like a small high saw over the sound of the waves. "Your wife's atman will flow into the open sea and from there into the next life. Water is all embracing. It will break any and all remaining attachment between atman and physical body. You may say few words for your peace of mind but not strictly necessary as per Hindu scripture."

A few words, yes, yes, why not? How many were a few in any case, four or six or five? Come up with a few words to communicate the infinite and the unsayable. What was more inadequate or disappointing or futile than a few words? When there was so much to say, why say anything? And where to start? Considering the improvised nature of the funeral at sea and the reluctant mourners-in-waiting and his own shaky hold on the moment, what could he say that would amount to anything? Why say the obvious, that the only difference between the living bodies on the boat and his wife was the most negligible difference of all, a question of carbon and recycling? That the smallest of events separated those on the boat from the one immersed, a fall, the flu, a random act of stupidity or malice. In any case, it seemed to Ullis that Niranjan had already said all that needed to be said. The sea dissolved the ties between the soul and the body. Attachment, attraction, all of it dissolved. Aki, free at last to slip this bloody coil and flow into her final shape.

"Just say something, it doesn't have to be a speech, you know," said Brinda. "You don't have to write a book. Say something about the five stages of grief and all, just say. Anger, violence, negotiation, nirvana, so on, so on."

She said this and Ullis heard the hollow boast of nitwit expertise. Poor Brinda's experience was more limited than she realised. How was she to know there were no stages? The neat categorisation appealed only to those, like Brinda, who had never known grief. (Though how was it possible to get to a certain age without experiencing grief in some way? How insulated or disconnected would you have to be?) The Kübler-Ross model was exactly that: a model. It didn't apply to real life. It was designed for the classroom and the seminar, an entire laughable thesis built around the idea that the dying had the presence of mind to proceed chronologically from denial to acceptance. The model had nothing to do with the living, who would spend the rest of their lives trying to process a single commonplace event. For whom the notion of *stages* did not exist. For whom there was no timeline, no demarcation, no five easy movements ending in some kind of Zen acceptance and forgiveness. No stages but an infinite spectrum, a thousand adjustments without an end in sight. Nothing here was linear or chronological. There was no beginning and no end, you moved back and forth like a time tourist, at sea without a compass, nothing above you but the tearful glimmer of the stars.

Grief, like time, is circular.

Besides, Brenda, I *am* writing a book.

Finally, all out of patience, Brinda snapped, "Chalo, let's go." She sat down with her handbag clutched in her lap and rummaged for cigarettes. Barefoot, her feet resting lightly on the wood slats, relaxed for the first time all evening.

The boat moved beneath a congealed teal sky. Salt spray stung their faces as they passed the last of the vessels anchored near Alibag and motored in charcoal light through deeper water. The spray carried a faint smell of fish and marigolds. Sudden lights swam out of the night, shadows rising out of the water like a ghost town on stilts. As they neared, the shadows resolved into giant rigs on iron supports drilled deep into the seabed. The boat slowed to navigate the narrow spaces in between. Ullis read the names as they passed, Noble Ed Holt and Dynamic Vision. Noble Ed was many hundreds of feet across, the size of a small city block. And like a city it was full of lights and noise, though it was a place without humans or conversation or commerce of any kind.

Unreal city, thought Ullis, city of my dreams.

Jagdish adjusted course away from the open sea, and the engine noise became deeper. The salt receded, replaced by the raw smell of sewage and marigolds. Small waves of heat touched Ullis's face. He saw bits of plastic in the water, empty Frooti cartons, packs of Benson & Hedges and Gold Flake, drinking straws, fast food wrappers, unidentifiable debris. Plastic waste and filth: they were nearing the city.

If he was to say something it should be now, and if not now then never. The boat moved haltingly forward. He felt a small shudder of relief and melancholy, the deep undertow of promises made and the mixed release of letting go. And what was he letting go? Only memory. Only history.

He found his phone and sent Aki a text. "I did it! I put ur ashes in fast water." He thought of scrolling up and reading her last messages. He had seen them only once, when she texted him on the night of her death, but now he couldn't remember what they said. Blessedly his mind had blanked. He would read them when he was able. First he would need a measure of fortification.

All of a sudden he had a bold craving for meow meow, a craving so real he could taste the chemical burn at the back of his throat. He wanted it now, the way it shut up the voices in his head and left him passed out for long moments before he came to. He could think of no pleasanter way of spending time than passing out and coming to, in lieu of sleeping and waking. He could think of no better way of bludgeoning the mind, which had an unpleasant habit of taking off in any old direction and returning always to the questions with no answer.

For instance to their last argument, Aki's voice low and steady because she did not shout, no matter what the provocation. The more angry or upset she was, the more controlled her voice. He heard her now: *You said I should never tell my dreams.* Had he actually told her this? That she should not tell him her dreams? What a monstrous thing to say to your wife, the person closest to you in the world. What had he been thinking? That life would go on for ever and there was plenty of time to sort things out, particularly with one's spouse. But to say such a thing! It was unforgivable, injurious, blasphemia in the Greek: to injure and to speak. He had blasphemed against his wife, against affection, against nature, and this last brought to mind the dandy J. K. Huysmans, whose blasphemies were calculated to cause maximum outrage, who therefore could be forgiven. For Dominic Ullis there would be no forgiveness. His crime was beyond forgiveness. His wife was dead because of his fatal inaction. How could he be absolved? He didn't deserve it. Without forgiveness there could be no healing, and if there was no healing then self-destruction was assured, even welcome. Which brought him back where he had started, with a sudden craving for meow meow that might be assuaged with measured doses of cocaine and/or heroin.

Buffeted by accustomed waves of guilt and regret, Ullis stood at the stern and gripped the handrails. He was facing the wrong way. He was turned towards the past, from where no relief would be forthcoming. The boat scraped against the landing dock and the Gateway of India loomed above them like the Victorian gate of hell. And there behind it was the red dome of the Taj. Tonight more than ever he thought the Gateway could do with an inscription reminiscent of *abandon all hope, ye who enter here*, but better suited to Bombay, something that rhymed, ending perhaps with the Italian proverb he had once heard and roughly translated as, 'Eat well, defecate prodigiously / Have no fear of death, or the deathly', something along the lines of:

This way to the grieving city,
This way to the districts of fear,
Where nothing lives except pity.
Remember this if you enter here:

Mangia molto, caca forte,
Nia paura de la morte.

Captain Juggie accepted his substantial payment and said, as if he had rehearsed it, "I am so sorry for your loss."

Before he stepped off the boat, Ullis handed over the backpack with the Jim Beam logo.

"Here," he said, "a keepsake of the night."

They clambered up the steep black steps that led from the water to the monument, carefully, because the stone was still wet from high tide. Brinda went first, clutching her handbag in one hand and her shoes in the other, her cigarette holder clenched between her teeth, stepping carefully on the uneven stone, Ullis next, stealing a glance at the boat, at the backpack and the box inside, which was an emblem in his mind of his wife's next-to-final resting place, and Niranjan last, talking softly in Marathi into a silver cell phone, which, as Ullis would learn, was something he liked to do a lot.

Jagdish settled down to wait. The weekend was the best part of his working week. As long as he was patient they would come, the Alibaggers looking for the last boat home, the late-night revellers who didn't want to taxi the long way round, a road trip of two and a half hours instead of twenty minutes on the water. He worried that it had been days since he'd uploaded a new video on his YouTube channel, the best free advertising in the world. He had planned to use his Samsung to videotape the trip he'd just made, because the three passengers looked respectable and important. He was about to ask them if it was okay to film the ride when the man in the suit asked him to stop the boat. What was supposed to be a joyride became the opposite, a funeral ride. What a good thing he hadn't filmed it! He lifted the backpack in his hand and felt the weight of the unlucky box and looked for a rubbish bin. But the passengers were still standing under the Gateway, as if they weren't used to the sensation of land under their feet.

"We can drop you," said Brinda to Ullis. "We're parked right here at the Yacht Club."

Brinda's brittle British accent and upper-class persona had its entertaining deaf spots. She pronounced yacht as *yatch-it* and it made her suddenly endearing.

"Would you like that?"

But dropped where? Where was he to go? What was he to do? He looked at his clasped hands. What would he do with his hands? Make a line the first chance he got, what else.

"Yes," he said. "I don't see why not."

"Come on," said Niranjan, putting away his cell phone. "This way. You will meet my trusty chariot!"

CHAPTER TWELVE

Scrolling Facebook on his phone, Ullis watched a video of the orange-skinned president's latest attacks on the brown-skinned, the yellow-skinned, the red-skinned and the black-skinned. The president talking to a group of reporters on the lawns of the White House, his awkward body language, the way he tugged at his jacket to hide his breasts, the way his tie hung low to hide his belly: how uncomfortable he was in his own skin, and how endearing. The overtanned bloviator's barefaced falsehoods, his thin skin and fear of mockery, these were the qualities that made him lovable. He was everyman. Unlike other politicians, he was not ashamed to let his insecurity show, and the corruption and the lies (which meant the lies were a form of truth-telling: he was saying, *I'm the president, I lie, it's part of the job*). His true mission was to undo the world and start over. Ullis understood the need to burn down the house, the country, the planet, and though he had no wish to destroy purely for the sake of destruction, purely to watch his ego at play, he understood this president. He dreaded the day the old mobster finally left office. What would happen then? Who could fill the blob-shaped hole in one's life? What could replace the addle-brained fuck trinket's daily episodes of reality television? It was too frightful to contemplate.

Niranjan's chariot was parked in Pasta Lane, Colaba's oldest and leafiest precinct. The white Audi had its sunroof open and windows up and the air conditioning on high. Dominic Ullis sat in the front passenger seat and replayed the president's press conference on the White House lawns. More and more it seemed a commemoration of the Age of Apocalypse. When the video came to an end, he looked up Nostradamus's quatrains and found a site that numbered and categorised them by the hundred, each hundredweight of quatrains gathered into a century. In Century III, Quatrain 81 he found what he was looking for, a striking description of the orange anti-Christ:

> The great shameless, audacious bawler,
> He will be elected governor of the army:
> The boldness of his contention,
> The bridge broken, the city faint from fear.

As he scrolled through the centuries he found other prophecies, imprecise but accurate, that described the cities of the world shaken by earthquakes and pummelled by tsunamis, riven by hunger and warfare and migration, beset by the rising waters of a heated planet. The sixteenth-century physician had mentioned the countries of Europe and Asia by name, though some names carefully omitted a single letter. The United Kingdom figured in a couplet:

> The great Britain including England
> Will come to be flooded very high by waters

Ullis was marking the site for future reference when Niranjan returned from his furlough, smelling of citrusy aftershave. He'd exchanged his white kurta-pyjamas for an identical pair, spotless, the creases intact. What else had he done upstairs? Tucked in Brinda with a cup of hot cocoa, taken a power nap, played a game of internet chess? He'd been away for half an hour and seemed ready now for a night on the town.

"Since I have deposited Brinda to home I am free bird." He slipped into the driver's seat. "Where you would like to be transported?"

In truth there was nowhere Ullis wished to go. He would have liked to sit in the car for ever with his itinerary in someone else's hands. He would have liked to make no decisions other than the most frivolous.

"I'm a free bird too," said Ullis, "flightless but free. And my schedule is clear."

"Good, good," said Niranjan. "We must go for drive. So much to do, so less time."

They sped through busy midnight streets, Niranjan proving to be an aficionado of acceleration and the grinding clutch. He drove as if the brake pedal was an inconvenience better ignored. He bore down on pedestrians and animals and vehicles as if they were elements in a video game. As he drove, he spoke softly via headphone and mouthpiece into the silver cell phone now resting on a holder on the dashboard.

"Niranjan," Ullis began.

"One minute," said Niranjan, ending the call. "You know what Niranjan means?"

"It means, let's see, pure, the pure one?"

"Correct," said Niranjan. "Call me Ninja, but. I'm not so pure these days."

"Ninja, it's very kind of you to give me a lift. But do you mind slowing down a little? I feel very slightly carsick."

Niranjan nodded reassuringly without slowing in the least. They came to a stretch of wet road near Bellasis Bridge, where a pipe had burst or a water tanker had disgorged its entire load. The Audi powered through a sunken patch, sending up a spray, its headlights shining wetly on small piles of gravel near the bridge. Through the sunroof Ullis glimpsed broken-down buildings teetering precariously. There was a glimpse of inky sky and no stars.

"Yes my friend, you will call me Ninja. What will I call you?"

"Whatever you want. It doesn't matter to me."

"Okay, then I call you Widow Boy. Now listen, do you trust me?"

Ullis considered the question of trust. It occurred instinctively and fully. Either you did or you did not. Niranjan was a politician and a gangster. He drove too fast. He wore rings on all his fingers. He was not the kind of person to inspire trust in anyone.

"Yes," Ullis answered truthfully, "I think I do."

"Good," said Niranjan. "I like you, Widow Boy, because you have the honest face. Don't worry, nothing bad can happen now. I am here."

He accelerated around a corner and narrowly skirted a handcart of bananas covered with a tarpaulin sheet.

"I am exceedingly safe driver, okay?"

"Okay," said Ullis.

Of course he was right. Nothing bad could happen because the worst had occurred. There was no reason to worry, now or in the future. *No worst, there is none. Pitched past pitch of grief . . .*

"Okay!" said Niranjan in a thick growl, as he sped past Marine Lines Station.

It was late but the streets were full of life. Lone drunk men dragged themselves home. Pavement families had their cook fires going and bedding spread for the night. The daytime traffic had thinned out, leaving the streets to the night birds, the birds of paradise and the birds of prey.

Somewhere deep in the grimy innards of Tardeo, Niranjan made a sudden right into a dark side street. He hadn't turned on his indicator lights and a Cheetah bike came to a squealing halt beside them. The Cheetah riders were the most demanding of all the cops, as if the painted motorbikes entitled them to a better standard of bribes. The policeman put his Cheetah on the stand and approached at leisure, hitching up his khakis. When he saw Niranjan the saunter became an energetic salute, followed by a grovelling bow and retreat.

They were outside a bar named Jungle Beats.

"One minute," Niranjan said, "I have some business inside, okay!"

"What kind of business? May I come along?"

"Business is business. I am family man. Just now when I went to home? What do you think I was doing?"

"Changing your clothes, I don't know. Freshening up?"

"No, no, completely wrong! I was checking up on my children."

"That's very nice, Ninja. I don't know what else to say."

"One boy, one girl. See, two children means expensive! Food expensive. Education expensive. So I am here past midnight, doing business to take care of home. You have children?"

"No," said Ullis.

"Usually I don't trust the men with no issues," Niranjan said, narrowing his eyes. "Why you don't like children?"

"I like children," said Ullis. "I think I like them more than grown-ups. Why do you like children?"

"I don't like children, only my children. Them, I love! Without

173

children where is the hope? Why I should work hard? What will I do with property and monies? Take to heaven?"

"So this is the reason to have children. Somewhere to leave your money and your house."

"No, no. That is added benefit," said Niranjan. "Maybe it's lucky you don't have. You cannot raise kids alone. Wife is important to life!"

It was never a question of luck. Aki didn't want children. This was one of the few things she was categorical about. Ullis had never questioned it, until one evening in Delhi when they went to a dinner party thrown by friends who had just had a baby.

She spends most of the evening hula hooping. She is an expert from the first try. Her hips move as if they are independent of the rest of her, and the hoop stays in the air of its own accord, as if it is attached to her waist and not to gravity. She wears the hoop like an accessory, casually, comfortably. She wears it like her flowery dress. With a small shock he notices the smile on her face. This is an important point; she so rarely smiles and now she is smiling involuntarily, without a trace of self-consciousness. He understands that for once she isn't thinking or overthinking. She is all body, no mind. As she works the hoop a small crowd gathers. They too seem hypnotised because they know how rare a moment it is. Or they are drawn to the sight of a girl in a summer dress lost in an ancient dance. She hoops the hula in time to the music, T. Rex's 'Bang a Gong', and at the moment when the singer whispers *You're dirty sweet and you're my girl* she turns towards Ullis. She is a light source running on joy. Everybody in the room can feel it and everybody feeds off the rhythm. She raises her arms and closes her eyes and then the hostess enters with the baby on her hip.

Now Aki steps out of the hoop and hands it to a friend. She is introduced to the baby. From this moment she forgets the dance and the party and her husband. He watches her cooing to the infant, carrying her, coming up with expressions that will make her laugh. He sees how patient she is, a natural mother. He has never seen this side of her and he feels obliged to mention it on the way home.

"You loved the baby," he says.

"I don't know if I believe in love at first sight," says Aki. "I think you need at least two meetings. Of course *we* were an exception to this rule. But then we're an exception to all rules."

"Who ever loved that loved not at first sight?"

"I'm impressed by the way you casually quote Shakespeare," she says seriously. "It's such an effective seduction technique."

"It isn't Shakespeare. He was quoting poor Christopher Marlowe."

"Ooh," she says. "You're dirty sweet and you bang my gong."

"I think we should think about it, considering you like children and they like you. Or we shouldn't think about it. We should take the plunge."

"I have thought about it," she says.

"And?"

"And yes I like babies, but that doesn't mean I want my own. I mean, why would you bring a baby into this?"

She gestures at the Imperial city. They are driving along a stretch of grim littered roadway. Dust-heavy trees cling to the verge and the railing has collapsed into the sidewalk. Outside a hospital a man has set up a tea stall. A woman in a wheelchair, wrapped in blankets, lifts a steaming plastic cup to her face. Ullis holds tight to the steering wheel as the car's front left tyre hits a pothole.

"It could be worse," he says. "It could be daytime. At least at night the poison is invisible."

"We must be grateful for all mercies, tiny and small."

"Yes."

"Especially small."

"It would be a small and beautiful baby," he says gamely.

"And what about after I'm gone? What happens to the beautiful baby then?"

"Everybody goes. All the more reason."

"Whatever," she says. "But the planet only has about twelve years. Twelve more years and life as we know it is over."

This is the prophecy she makes, words he will remember in the years to come.

"Twelve years."

"Yes. Why bring a child into a dying system? And by the way? It isn't true that the poison is invisible at night. Take a look at that. What do you think it is? Mist?"

"Why are you so angry?"

"I don't want children. You're with the wrong girl. I have many objections to the baby game."

"Well, now would be the time to air them."

"Toru Dutt, Amy Winehouse, Katharine Hepburn, Emily Dickinson, Eva Perón, Anaïs Nin, Meena Kumari, Amrita Sher-Gil. You see what I mean, Dommie?"

"What do you mean, Aki?"

"My heroes are child-free. It was such a liberating realisation for me, to know I don't have the maternal instinct and I don't have the narcissist's instinct. I suspect they're the same thing."

She is silent for a long time. The noxious city slides past the window. On the wide sidewalk outside a government college, a family has constructed a tent made of plastic sheeting. The young father cooks something in a tin pot turned white from repeated scrubbing. When she speaks, her voice is calm and even, without anger and without affection.

"The truth is I'm not going to inflict my lack of maternal feeling on a baby," she says. "Can't you see how helpless they are? I'm not going to do it, Dommie, look at what happened to me."

And then he remembers what she told him at their first meeting, the wanting to die, and he understands what she is getting at, that she does not want children because she does not believe in the future. She does not want to bring a baby into a world that might end at any moment, because she would be a suicidal mom biding her time and sooner or later the child would be motherless, and he understands that they are in an elevator falling to the ground many floors below amid a shower of sparks and screams. They never talk about children again.

Jungle Beats was a concrete-fronted establishment that appeared shut for the night. Then the security man saw Niranjan and pulled the shutters to reveal a noisy interior lit by dim yellow bulbs. There were men packed half a dozen to a table, served by women in salvaar kameez. On one side was a beer dispenser from which came most of the light in the room. Hindi music blared muddily. The air conditioning was loud and faulty, and smoke hung in the air like a thick horizontal curtain. From behind the cash counter, a man emerged to greet Niranjan and touch his sandal-clad feet. "Welcome, saheb," he said, and ushered them into an inner room bigger and darker than the one they entered.

On a small stage, a woman in a diaphanous green sari danced to 'Hamma Hamma' from the movie *Bombay*. She mimed disinterestedly to the complex words and music, as if she had done it many times before and couldn't be bothered to pretend she enjoyed it. During the more difficult phrases she gave up the mime altogether. She stood still and framed her face with her hands and tilted her head from side to side, moving very little but with great self-assurance, sometimes flexing only her shoulders, sometimes only her feet. At tables around the stage, the men sat alone drinking beer or whisky. They gazed at her with the rapt expression of the devotee. A young broker or small businessman went to the stage, and with a practised flick of his wrist a bundle of new fifty-rupee notes showered crisply around her. She did not deign to notice the money or the eager young punter, except with a single disapproving glance. After a while he returned to his seat, watched by a bouncer who stood in the shadows near the stage. The dancer's green chiffon sari draped a slender figure. The hands framing her face were small and perfectly formed. It was the first time in weeks that Ullis had admired someone's hands. It may not have been desire exactly but it was close enough. It might have been sense memory, an ache in a phantom limb. The fact that it had returned brought a fresh wave of perplexed guilt. The body's fleshy mechanisms and endless nostalgia – was there no end to its indignities?

Niranjan led the way to an inner room, a low-ceilinged pit with fake leather booths and mirrored tables. This room too was badly lit, but candles were burning and the music had been turned low. A hostess showed them to a table. As soon as they were seated drinks appeared, a selection of whisky and brandy and a battered bucket of ice. A waiter put down mineral water and bowls of roasted peanuts. Another produced a pad and pencil. The air was stale and smelled of old beer.

"Bring food," said Niranjan.

Food! Ullis's stomach heaved at the thought. There was really only one way to handle food-related queasiness, and that was with a quick line of cocaine supplemented by a slow line of heroin. It was a way of protecting oneself from future uneasiness. He got up and excused himself.

"Sit down," said Niranjan, words that always made Ullis want to flee. "You are wanting drugs, correct?"

"Yes."

"You may consume here only. There is nothing to worry."

"Oh, there's lots to worry, just not for you," said Ullis.

Niranjan looked at him expressionlessly for a long time.

Then he said, "You are making joke, correct?"

"Correct."

Expressionlessly Niranjan said, "Ha."

Drugs taken at a restaurant in full view of waiters and patrons – it was almost like the old days. When heroin was an unknown quantity, you were free to snort and shoot and smoke wherever you liked. You would be spot-chasing brown on a bench at the railway station, and by the time the general public realised something was afoot you were gone. The enterprisingly named Paradise Cafe in Mahim even provided needles and assorted works in a cup on each table. You used the candle thoughtfully provided on a saucer. You boiled up a fix and took your shot. Then you nodded out over a Fanta or a Mangola. HIV and HCV were unknown acronyms, and the idea of blood-borne terminal ailments had never occurred to recreational drug users. It was very likely that one of those communal needles was the asp he had taken to his breast, the gift that kept on giving, the virus that raised its head some twenty-five years later to bite him in the liver.

What happened to Paradise? For many years he associated that stretch of the Mahim Causeway with the idea of paradise as a place beyond the reach of propriety or the law. But when a small army of stoned young men and women started frequenting the cafe, the police demanded so much hafta that the proprietors had to shut it down. It reopened as a conventional coffee shop though some artefacts remained. The pale turmeric walls and the soot smears from a thousand junkie candles made for a spooky palimpsest, layers of elongated shadows like the silhouettes of ghosts.

On his last trip to the city, he took a detour to Mahim and kept the cab waiting while he tried to find the location of the old cafe. The building was the same but his memory could no longer be relied upon. Instead of the circular iron staircase that led to the residential floors above, he found a wall plastered with political posters. Around the corner, a cell phone showroom and a dry-cleaner's. The cigarette vendor had disappeared and so had the tree under which he had plied his trade. It was as if the entire corner had been obliterated and every trace of its personality erased. He was impressed by the ferocity with which the new Bombay devoured the corpse of the old. History was always being paved over and renovated and corrected. The city did not care about its previous lives and it did not care about the lives to come, it cared only about the life it was living.

Praising what is lost makes the remembrance dear. Which corner of his dented consciousness had thrown up that line? Was it a fragment from a poem, a movie, a greeting card, or had it dropped from the blue? In any case, he had no wish to make remembrance any dearer than it was. It's already dear, dearie, thank you very much. When he surrendered to memory, he felt like a small planet trying to resist the pull of the black hole Aki. All remembrance led to her. Flight was futile and it always ended the same way, on his own, craving to be emptied into a dull opiate from the eighteenth century, craving camphorated paregoric, or tincture of laudanum, or any kind of blessed oblivion.

He spilled a bit of cocaine on his wrist, and was rolling up a note one-handed when Niranjan made a gesture and a bouncer gave him a metal straw. He snorted quickly and returned the straw.

"What about me?" said Niranjan.

The dancer in the diaphanous green chiffon and a tall bald man came to the table. Niranjan waved at them to sit and turned back to Ullis.

"What?" he said. "I don't get?"

He made a strange gesture to the bouncer. Cupping his hand in the air, he rotated his fingers as if he were changing a light bulb. Then he nodded at the only other table that was occupied, three men quietly drinking beer and eating kebabs. The bouncer said something to them and they left the room. Niranjan stretched out a hand, his fat beringed fingers spread wide, and Ullis gave him the baggie with his depleted stash. He winced as the last of the cocaine was crushed and snorted in a mighty sniff. The bald man watched impassively as Niranjan flung the mirror on the table and clapped his hands.

"More," he said. "More!"

Waiters brought brandy in a snifter and a jug of orange juice. Niranjan put ice in the brandy and half filled the snifter with juice. He drank without touching his lips to the glass.

"Niranjan seth," said the dancer teasingly. "You always want more. Isn't it true?"

Niranjan shrugged and straightened the rings on his fingers.

"Who is the friend you brought to see me?" said the dancer.

"This is Ullis, Englishwallah hain," he said apologetically, as if Ullis's language relegated him to a remote and disagreeable region of hell. "Ullis, this is the great Meena Kumari."

"Meena?" said Ullis, politely shaking hands. He tried to keep the disbelief out of his voice. "Meena Kumari?"

"Mummy daddy fans thi," she said and went back to her phone.

"And this is Sub-Inspector Dhabolkar," said Niranjan.

He made his fingers into a pistol and pointed at the stocky bald man, who nodded and said nothing. Dhabolkar's shirt was loose over his jeans and he wore a baseball cap to hide his eyes. Reaching into his hip pocket, he retrieved a thick office envelope held together with a rubber band. He offered the envelope with both hands. Niranjan put it away without looking inside.

"Dhabolkar used to be theatre actor on Marathi stage," said Niranjan. "I convinced him to join second most dramatic of all the professions, police."

"Which is most dramatic, Niranjan sir?" asked Meena Kumari.

"Politics is most!" said Niranjan. "Even more than dancing."

He downed the rest of his brandy and orange juice in his finicky way, by holding the snifter some distance from his lips and letting the drink fall into his mouth. Then he stood up and shook hands with Ullis.

"You can stay as long as you want," he said as he left, followed obediently by Dhabolkar. "I will see you, Widow Boy! Meena, walk with me to my transportation."

Ullis was sorry to see Niranjan leave, which made him wonder at his new sentimentality. Was this what happened to someone who came home one day to find his wife hanging from a ceiling fan, who tried to breathe life into her lungs and failed? Did such a person begin to see the living as brief and wondrous apparitions, each worthy of affection and attention, whether a chance acquaintance on an airplane, or a stranger dancing in a bar, or an endearingly incompetent criminal president?

Meena returned a few minutes later and took her seat and snapped her fingers. A waiter appeared, looking frightened.

"Chivas Regal," she announced without looking up from her phone, and the waiter hurried away. When he returned with her drink she told him to fill the glass with ice and top it up with Coca-Cola.

"The name of this cocktail is *highball*," she said as she took a first sip. "Did you know that?"

Her English was fluent and unaccented, as if she had picked it up by watching television shows beamed from far-flung corners of the globe.

"I think I did know that," said Ullis.

"If this is a highball what is a lowball?"

"Indian whisky and Thums Up?"

Meena Kumari graced him with a small bored smile. Clearly she didn't think it was much of a joke.

"When Niranjan seth is here, girls do not drink in front of him," she said. "He does not like it. Actually he hates it."

"What does he like?" asked Ullis.

"What does he like?" and Meena Kumari laughed, a low-pitched sound that issued hesitantly and briefly from her wonderful mouth. "He likes Sati Savitris. Even girls in the bar line, he wants them to act like Mother India. I don't know why he calls me Meena Kumari. No, not true, I know why. He likes to say her name. I never saw a movie by her in my life. My friend told me she was a drunkard and her life was fully tragic. I think I look more like Manisha Koirala than Meena Kumari. What do you think?"

"Manisha Koirala definitely."

"Manisha also drinks, but not as much as Meena. My real name is Tamanna."

"Tamanna."

"Yes. It is the name I gave myself. Isn't it nice?"

"Very nice," said Ullis.

She looked at him doubtfully and went back to her phone. Which reminded Ullis that he had an urgent text to send because Niranjan had unilaterally annexed his cocaine. He typed: "Need to see u. ASAP?" Putting the phone away, he patted his inner jacket pocket to check that the h-dash-in was still there. His phone vibrated. It was Danny with a quick reply: "Now m busy bru. Lucky's at 6 a.m.?" Ullis texted: "OK".

And since he had his phone out, he sent a text to his wife: "Trying to 4give but ur not helping. Nothing helps. M not sure why."

Waiters arrived bearing platters of kebabs and onions with fresh mint and hot rotis and cut watermelon. They placed plates on the table and started to serve the food but Tamanna waved them away. She wanted to serve him with her own hands. As she piled his plate with choice pieces of fruit and meat, she helped herself to small morsels. Prettily she wiped watermelon juice from her lips. Like Meena Kumari and Manisha Koirala, courtesans of the highest temperament, Tamanna's eyes were large and liquid and doomed. They were her most prominent feature, followed closely by tragedienne's cheekbones. She looked as if she might expire at any moment from a forgotten nineteenth-century ailment.

"Excuse me," she said as she squeezed lime on a morsel of lamb. "I think you must be a poet?"

"I'm really not," he said, recoiling. "Why do you say such a thing?"

"You are beautiful and sorrowful like all the poets," she said. "My favourite beautiful poet is the great Sahir Ludhianvi. He was born in Punjab like me."

"I'm sorry that I don't know his work."

"Do you know the song 'Main Pal Do Pal Ka Shayar'?"

"Yes, I do," he said, surprised. "Is that Sahir Ludhianvi?"

Tamanna nodded happily. And a memory came to him: Guru Dutt's accursed poet standing in a narrow doorway as the light streamed around his shoulders, his arms spread in the pose of the crucified Christ. It was a false memory, the wrong Hindi melodrama and the wrong actor. But he remembered the words clearly enough to translate: "*I am the poet who will last for a moment or two.*"

"I knew it," she said, her great eyes shining. "You are a poet. But why did Niranjan sir call you widow boy?"

"I'm sure he has his reasons," said Ullis. "Niranjan is a man of means and mystery."

"He mentioned that you lost your wife."

"Lost implies a possibility of finding."

"How did she expire?"

"Milk expires. My wife died."

"It was natural causes or susside?"

"Forgive me, I'll be back in a moment," said Ullis, getting up.

He went in search of a bathroom. Fortification was surely in order – if not now then never again. Tamanna's questions were too insistent and too close to the bone in his current state of sudden unintended sobriety. And now that Niranjan was no longer around, he wasn't comfortable taking drugs in a dance bar full of cops and crooks. He tripped over a wooden partition and found the bathroom at the end of a corridor screened by a filthy floral curtain. It was crowded with young men primping at the mirrors. He found an empty cubicle and shut the door and carefully spilled a spot of heroin on his phone. He would have chased it with a spot of cocaine if there was any left.

Thanks, Ninja, for finishing my C.

Back at the table he ordered more whisky. Some of the other tables were filling up again. Tamanna gestured to a small dance floor where three women in gagra cholis danced slowly to the hit song 'Kajra Re'. Unlike Tamanna, they used hand gestures borrowed from hip-hop and Bharata Natyam. Unlike Tamanna, they made lots of eye contact with the men in the room. One got up with a garland of five hundred-rupee notes which he placed around the neck of the main dancer, who, in Ullis's opinion, was nowhere close to Tamanna's level of hauteur.

"You're so much better," he said.

"I think so," she said. "This is your first time at Jungle Beats, no?"

"So it is," he said, remembering banter as something he'd been good at. "Have you been dancing here a long time?"

She regarded him speculatively.

"I'll tell you one story," she said. "You are a poet. You will understand. Once I was on a bus. I was wearing a simple sari, not

186

like this dinchak green chiffon. I was a simple girl wearing simple sari going to simple job. The bus was crowded and I had to push. I was in the entryway when the bus started to move and then a man pushed in behind me. He was standing so close I could feel his entire body. I tried to move ahead but he stayed stuck. This man is a scoundrel, I thought. He is a rascal. I turned around and slapped him. Loudly, I slapped. The whole bus turned to look. The man's sunglasses fell off and he started to cry. Then I saw he was blind. He was carrying a cane and everything. I felt bad but not too much. Blind or not, he deserved the slap. After all, he was a man. Now the other people on the bus started shouting at me. He's blind, they said. Why did you slap a blind man? He doesn't know anything, poor fellow. They shouted at me and I shouted back. But I was not confident in those days. I was a schoolteacher. I got down at the next stop and walked all the way to my work. I promised to myself I will never take the bus again. Soon after that I came to Jungle Beats for a job."

"Who wouldn't," said Ullis. "Dancing is a better option. At least you can take taxis."

"I don't take taxis, no thank you. I have my own car and driver."

"But that's even better," said Ullis.

Tamanna smiled and dreamily nodded. Her fringed gold earrings swung back and forth like miniature sun umbrellas.

"Bilkul," she said, "but this line is only good for a short time. It is good to make money when a girl is young. Later when she is older there's no future." She got up and smoothed the waist of her salvaar. She took a small sip of her drink and yawned delicately. Her mouth made a perfect O. "Now I dance. It is my last shift. You will wait for me?"

"I have to go."

"Really? You're really going?"

"Yes," he said, also getting up.

"You don't want to stay with me?"

"I'd like to, but I have to meet my friend Danny."

Tamanna shook her head. She looked unblinkingly at him with her doomed beseeching eyes. Between her brows was a red-and-black bindi in the shape of a young tree. He noticed that her upper lip was fuller than her lower lip and both her lips were red, though she did not wear lipstick.

Chastely, carefully, he shook her hand.

CHAPTER THIRTEEN

On his way out, the man at the counter refused to give him a bill. "Nahi, nahi," he said, putting up his hands like someone showing his wounds. At least he didn't try to touch Ullis's feet. Instead he bowed and said, "Niranjan sahib," as if he were taking the name of the Lord of the Meeting Rivers. When the security man pulled the shutter closed, the noise of the bar faded in an instant. From the outside Jungle Beats offered a bland and innocent facade. You might think it was a clothing boutique. Only if you listened carefully did you hear the ribald folk percussion of 'Kajra Re' playing repeatedly through the evening because it was a favourite of the bar girls. Only if you stood under the dark awning of that jewellery store across the street did you see the young men emerge drunk, their hearts hollowed out by devotion, every last hundred-rupee note showered on a distant dancer. He would have liked to see Tamanna ply her skills once more, but what was the point? Watching her dance was pleasure and pain in equal measure. At the moment and for the foreseeable future, he was only in the market for pain and its periodic alleviation by the judicious use of synthetic painkillers.

He set off along the deserted street in what he hoped was the direction of the main road. As always when walking in South Bombay, past buildings constructed more than two hundred years earlier, he felt a sense of continuity and serenity that was absent in the daytime when the air was full of noise and confusion. In the quiet hours before dawn, it was possible to believe that the city was a site of human history rather than the history of commerce, a place created for the movement of people rather than the movement of money.

He passed an entire joint family on the narrow sidewalk. Old people and small children lay unguarded in sleep, their wide-open arms indicating trust or foolhardiness. There was a sleeping dog curled into a tight bundle. There were clothes hanging from a railing. There was scattered bedding and blackened pots and a plastic bucket with a piece missing from the rim. He saw the smoking remnants of a cook fire. Against a slender tree, a pile of school clothes and a lean-to made of discarded tin. He passed taxis and handcarts parked haphazardly, as if their owners had left in a great hurry. In the middle of the road was a single leather shoe. Somewhere close, dogs were barking. Where was he, Tardeo or Opera House or Ballard Estate? Or an abandoned neighbourhood in a town hit by catastrophe?

Near the awning of a second-hand newspaper shop he saw two figures crouched under a bed sheet. Around them the paraphernalia of the dragon chaser: burnt strips of tin foil and guttered candles and Gold Flake packets cut into strips. One of the men had an open matchbox under his big toe. From time to time he would extract a matchstick, scrape it along the box and heat a length of silver foil. He wore the aura of heroin like armour, oblivious to everything but the task at hand even as the city swarmed around him. Taking in the scene, Dominic Ullis experienced a jolt of nostalgia so powerful he felt pain in his sinuses. It struck him that the word nostalgia *was* indicative of pain, like neuralgia or myalgia. Not pain in the nerves or muscles or joints, but pain in the memory, a condition as draining as any other.

"May I sit here?" he said.

One of the men had nodded out, spectacularly, his forehead touching the road, his upper body curved into an improbable yoga. He wore high-waisted blue jeans and a mullet. The other man pulled a new matchstick from the box under his toe. The foil-covered tube in his mouth moved over a trace of sticky brown liquid. He inhaled with a hiss and there was no smoke. Ullis took a seat on the kerb and dug for the vial in his pocket. When he took it out a miracle occurred. Both men came awake, ever alert to the presence of good, possibly free gear.

"Kaunsa maal hai, bhai?" said the guy with the mullet.

"Ekdum first-class maal," said Ullis, without irony. "Aapka foil use kar saktha?"

"Hah, kyon nahi? Apne ko bhi dena, yaar!"

It wasn't exactly a fair exchange, good heroin for the use of some foil and a few matchsticks. But who was Ullis to demand satisfaction? The only satisfaction on offer was a streak of dirty brown melting on a strip of silver. He borrowed the toker and turned it around to the unused side and offered a silent prayer against communicable diseases. Putting a small hillock of powder on the foil, he lit a match and chased the wisp of smoke that ensued. He held the smoke in his lungs for long enough that nothing emerged when he exhaled. Then he repeated the procedure. He was showing off, for it had been a long time since he had chased the magic dragon.

The Genet formulation came to mind, as it sometimes did during heroinated or meowian moments. What was it exactly? That one was never reluctant to display one's underground skills in respectable company, even if one had long stopped using said skills. Or something along those lines – Genet of *The Thief's*

Journal, taking pride rather than shame in the tube of K-Y jelly among his possessions displayed on a policeman's desk. Ullis was not among the respectable at the moment, he was among the low. Not that low company was any less deserving of attention than high society, or any less appreciative of the skills one acquired in the pursuit of vice. He took some pride in wiping the foil clean and tapping out another careful mound of powder.

Passing the strip of silver to the man with the improbable hair, Ullis leaned against a handcart, its back at the exact angle an armchair would take. How comfortable it was, how smooth and welcoming the worn panels of wood against his head, how fine a resting place for a man with an infinitely renewable reserve of sleeplessness. All around him the crowded night glimmered like velvet among the angels and ghosts. His eyelids slammed shut and melted with images. The nod arrived heavy, rapturous. Aki in the sari she wore to the City Clerk's office in Manhattan, smiling at him on the day of their wedding, witnessed by random City Hall bureaucrats and unknown other brides and grooms. He remembered the weather vividly. A brilliant day in April and the smell of spring already in the air, the sky as blue as island water. As for this morning's weather, don't ask. He didn't have a clue.

He has so many questions for her.

"Did you like being married to me?"

"There was no question of liking," she says, shaking her finger at him. "I couldn't imagine not being married to you. I liked *marrying* you."

"You were so beautiful. You wore your sari with such attitude it made City Hall glamorous. I looked at you, the way you were glowing, and it crushed me. I thought: in thirty years I'll be old and creaky. She'll only be old. Why did she marry me?"

"I married you because men my own age bore me to tears. I wasn't interested in working so hard. I wanted the work already done, or at least half done. I wanted the rough edges nicely rounded. I didn't think twice. *We* didn't think twice. We jumped into it like it was a pool on a summer afternoon in Delhi. I was so happy. Until the last day, I was happy. Then it got out of hand a little bit. Didn't it?"

"A little bit? Are you out of your mind?"

"Obviously," she says, reaching for the goblet of red wine glowing like stained glass on the windowsill beside her. "This is what it means to be dead, you are subject to an out-of-body out-of-mind experience."

"You killed yourself," he says.

(As in all dreams there is a vivid thread of logic in the nod. Years later he will recall that his sense of grievance lasts throughout the exchange with the spirit or memory or revenant that is Aki. The fact of her death makes no difference to his great grievance against her. Her return from the dead brings no resolution. Ghost or hallucination, she is real and necessary as air. The conversation and its familiar currents of resentment and accusation will continue for the rest of his life.)

He attempts levity: "It was susside, a clear case of."

"It was a momentary lapse," she says, her untroubled gaze holding his. "I'd been angry all day after the argument in the car when I thought we were going to crash. I went out and met friends to punish you, because I didn't want to be there when you got back.

But I was the one who was punished. I got home and you weren't there. In all the time we were together, not once in four years had you not been home at night."

"I went out looking for you. I went to Humayun's Tomb. I thought you might be there, sitting on a bench, waiting for me. I called and called. You never picked up. I wandered around and ran into people I knew."

"I called you eventually. As soon as you answered I knew you weren't alone."

"I was in a car," he says. "There were people in the car. I couldn't talk freely. Sorry, I'm sorry."

"I heard them, women laughing. I knew they were laughing at me. And now I must tell you something."

"This is the strangest nod I've ever had. The strangest nod ever undertaken in the great republic of nod. They weren't laughing at you, Aki. They were dropping me home. I didn't take the car because I didn't trust myself to drive. I was on my way to you."

"I know you were."

"If only you'd waited a few minutes."

"Enough," she says, smiling. The window behind her fills with white light. "The tigers of wrath are not wiser than the horses of instruction. I learned too late."

"*The Marriage of Heaven and Hell*," he says, his literary references always on point. "But you reversed it."

Aki's smile shrinks to a tight seam.

"You must change your religion," she says. "Which is as easy or difficult as changing your mind. Become horse not tiger."

"Horse, h-dash-in," says Ullis, "the hero of heroin."

"If you quit drugs and alcohol where will it leave you?" she says. "Not with a drug- or booze-shaped hole, but with a God-shaped

hole in your heart. Quit quitting. Accept heroin as your new god.
Or better still, come with me."

"What?"

"Follow me, I'll take you."

She says this but her heart isn't in it. He can tell.

He came to with a start, his phone buzzing with a text from
Danny: "There in 10, see u." He stared at the message unseeing,
Aki's words ringing in his head. *Become horse not tiger.* It was
the opposite of Blake's dictum. The horses of instruction and
reason pulled in the opposite direction from the tigers of wrath
and instinct. Aki was saying follow reason. Follow the horse, not
h-dash-in. She was telling him *not* to take heroin. Had she had a
change of heart? Or had she been saying this all along and he'd
heard her wrong, deliberately, for his own reasons?

He was still staring at Danny's text. It took a long moment
for the words to register. There was no chance he would make
it across the city to Bandra in ten minutes, but Danny's ten
was an ordinary man's hour. He had plenty of time if he set off
immediately.

"Thoda tho dena, yaar," said one of the young junkies. His
attempted smile exposed front teeth crusted with a layer of brown
tar.

Ullis left a small helping of powder on the foil.

"What is your good name?" It was the junkie with the mullet.

"Dominic," he said. "And yours?"

"I am Sonu. Welcome to my home."

"It's very nice to meet you," said Ullis.

"Mujhe bhi," said Sonu.

He took a last drag and passed the foil to his friend. He said the stretch of sidewalk they were sitting on had been his home for almost a year now. A comfortable place, except during the monsoon. What did Ullis think of Bombay's monsoons?

"I find it hard to believe that people live here. It's uninhabitable for most of the year but the monsoons are murderous, the entire city flooded with filth," said Ullis, looking up at the clear night sky, alert to augury and fray. "It's unlivable yet people live here. It's true of everywhere, true and getting truer as the years pass. You can see it if you look for it. First the water rises slowly, so slowly it's imperceptible. But you know it's higher than it was last year. It's higher and you have to raise your house. You raise your house and then you raise it again. Now the water comes suddenly. Huge water, huge lakes, great rivers where it has always been dry. Flash floods in places that have never flooded before. Then the water doesn't come at all. It dries the earth, cracks it open. There are cracks where there was moisture, a new desert, and people become water refugees. They take their animals and move to the cities. But the city can't handle the influx. The riots begin, the killings, the long struggle, tribes forming and reforming, everybody living for the day, for the next few hours. It's already happening. It's already crazy that we live the way we live. Look at the huge fissures in the land and in the water. Think about earthquakes. Entire towns flattened overnight. Or washed away overnight. Your house shredding around you, your street washed away, your car floating upside down among the trees.

The permafrost thawing faster than anybody imagined, abruptly thawing over vast tracts of the Arctic, and the billions of tons of carbon that's locked into it, waiting to be released into the atmosphere, to make everything hotter. More heat, more water, more displacement. We say, how can this be? Yet we endure, year after year we endure. It's a natural calamity, we say. The hand of God is upon us but we take pride in our resilience. We shall overcome. We'll bounce back. But it's happening more often and it gets worse every time. And what do you do afterwards? Do you go back to the town or neighbourhood or village that has washed away or dried up? Do you try and reconstruct your life? How do you do it when the old world is gone? How do you live through the next catastrophe? How do you persist? How do you rebuild knowing it will happen again? You search the sky for clues, listen to the birds and the dogs for a warning, and you pick up and move on, go somewhere new to start again. Why do you do it? There's nowhere to go and everywhere is the same."

Sonu looked at Ullis for a moment in amazement. Then he nodded vigorously and nodded out, his forehead coming to rest on the sidewalk.

"Chalo, good night. I mean good morning," Ullis said politely, swaying in the direction of the traffic.

It was almost six and the crows were awake, making their usual outsize clamour. For how long had he nodded out? It felt like hours. On the sidewalk a woman stirred a great battered cauldron. There were benches to the side, already crowded with early morning tea drinkers waiting for the brew. The smell of strong tea boiled with milk was one of the smells he associated with the city, along with the smell of sewage and flowers. His stomach seized pleasantly. It occurred to him that he had kept some food down, the kebabs from Jungle Beats. Soon he'd be able to hold a glass of water, though this was always a bad sign. It meant you were getting accustomed to heroin, which in turn meant you were a beat away from the wild turkey of withdrawal and the many and varied pleasures of hell the wretched bird brought in her wake. If he *were* to change his religion, what shape would the new faith take? Was he shedding or acquiring? Quitting drugs – what an idea. How final and unaccommodating. Like being left without faith or protection in a pagan world. How newly opened to emotion it left you, your immunity to 'feelings' newly suspended. This was what it meant to kick drugs. You were kicking against God. It was a futile exercise.

He found a taxi waiting at the junction.

"Bandra," he said. "Thoda jaldi karna."

"You want to go from Sea Link?" said the driver in only slightly broken Bombay English. Ullis noted the seesaw rhythm and the emphatic tempo. Here it was, one of the great dialects of the world, in which English was bent and reshaped to fit the needs of the living city.

"Yes," he said, "please."

"Mujik?"

"Okay," said Ullis. "Thank you."

The driver put the radio on and turned down the volume and old Hindi music wafted into the car, a snatch of R. D. Burman, the composer in full orchestral mode with a knowing nod in the direction of jazz, those frantic violins over a battalion of congas, a man rhythmically panting...

Ullis settled back into the seat and wound down the window. Warm air blew into the car, bringing scents of night jasmine and cinders.

"Enjai," said the driver.

Was Bombay the only city in the country in which speaking English was not considered a subversive elitist activity? Perhaps, but it was also the city in which speaking English was considered a deeply subversive elitist activity. The city had changed its name. It had changed the names of streets, museums, government buildings, universities, airports, restaurants and libraries. Most recently Elphinstone Road Station, which shared its name with the college Ullis had taken pride in not attending, had had its name changed to Prabhadevi. The spree of renaming was the mark of a broken civilisation that hated English and aspired to it at one and the same time. Even the people in charge of the city, leaders of the current regime such as Niranjan, aka Ninja seth, took care to denigrate Englishwallahs in public while enjoying a westernised lifestyle in private. Prominent among them was the founder of the party who was still its spiritual head, the cartoonist turned demagogue who had changed his name from Thakré to Thackeray but insisted the city change its name in reverse, from Bombay to Mumbai.

Where would it all end except in the sea?

As they crossed the Sea Link, the day went from dark to bright in a single slow-motion sweep. The inky sky, shot through with streaks of pink and mauve, went to full day though the sun had not yet shown itself. It was as if someone had turned the dimmer on a chandelier without bothering about subtlety or atmosphere. He knew who that someone was. Winding down the window he shook his fist at heaven, which by now had revealed itself fully.

"Take it slow," he said aloud. "Let me catch my breath, why

don't you? I'm dizzy with the speed. Slow it down, you're going too fast."

"Not too fast," said the driver, "speed limit is eighty kph. See?"

He pointed at his speedometer, which hovered around seventy.

"I see nothing," said Ullis, echoing Schultz, a favourite childhood television character from a show about American prisoners of war who outwitted their foolish Nazi captors week after week. The show had been on his mind lately thanks to the new reality of America, the resurgence of blood and soil, the display of blond hair and polo shirts and burning torches, a fundamentally decent populace imprisoned and manipulated by charlatans, playing up the need for comedy in the face of its opposite.

He said: "I see *nothing*. I hear *nothing*. Most of all, I *know* nothing."

The ride passed in companionable silence.

All around him the city swarmed, the junkyard city with its million-dollar views of the junkyard, ahead of him the Palais Royale, newest and highest of high-rises, surrounded by slums on every side, an embodiment of the city's long-standing tryst with ugliness and wealth, the building's construction delayed while municipal officers extracted the largest bribes possible, around it a forest of other high-rises, grandiose exercises in excess, a secret society of unsold apartments in overpriced buildings, the neighbouring red-light district razed and remade into office towers, the street of opium dens and hashish parlours become travel agencies and retail emporia, the Soviet-era blocks of unbridled Brutalism beside nineteenth-century examples of genteel Victoriana, the whole breathtaking tumbledown palace taking shape now out of the early morning smog, all around him the glorious ash-heap of the city coming into view degree by unexpected degree, the abandoned textile mills converted into chic prefab nightspots, the tanneries razed and reconstructed into white-walled art galleries, the surviving docks and fisheries coming to life, entire neighbourhoods submerged under the smell of dry fish, the banyan and peepal trees turned into shrines with a bit of coloured fabric, a stub of lit candle, a smear of kumkum, the silk-cotton trees become homes for the homeless, every tree and corner and street and neighbourhood an endless gradation of caste and ghetto, the ocean of lower-middle, islands of upper-middle, and the ever-flowing river of middle-middle, the East Indian convention halls and doilied homes where elderly couples dance the twist, singing along to Jim Reeves and Cliff Richard, a print of blond blue-eyed Jesus above a perpetual candle in the living room, the young courting couples and married couples huddling in the dark on the seafront, trying for a moment of intimacy away from the eyes of joint families and predatory constables, the secret beach at Mahim and its dirty brown sand, the miles-long railway station market stalls already setting up to sell cheap underwear, pirated movies, sex toys, time-saving kitchen gadgets and fresh marigolds for the temple, the air-conditioned windowless rooms that exist beyond day or night where the figures on the couch are always interchangeable and the drugs on the coffee table cut with powdered milk and local anaesthetic, where a girl dances alone in the kitchen to music no one else can hear, music more basic than the 4/4 EDM playing in the rest of the house, and as the taxi sped past neighbourhoods he classified according to the drugs he had taken and the houses he had taken them in, the city became a catalogue of unstable highs and terrible lows, the years of addiction and withdrawal that marked his life before he met Aki one Saturday afternoon in Manhattan.

From the beginning of their time together, her great fear was that he would go back to heroin. Which carried a supplemental fear: if he went back to heroin he would leave her. In her mind heroin was a siren on the rocks, singing the love supreme. Heroin would pull him back with a single glance from her flashing eyes. On the day after the wedding at City Hall she woke him on their honeymoon bed in the honeymoon room at the Plaza, woke him early to tell him he must put down in writing his 'heartfelt assurance' that he'd never again use drugs.

There were many such undertakings during the brief course of their marriage and he was always touched by her childlike belief in the written word. Years later he would find them in the back pocket of notebooks, in sketchbooks, in files where odd pieces of paper had been secreted with documents that seemed important at the time. She did this knowing he would come across them one day when she was no longer around. And when he did he would pore over them, looking for clues, a key, maybe a code, something to unlock the puzzle that was Aki.

Once, in an old notebook, he found this on the back of a customer receipt for an interim licence from the New York Department of Motor Vehicles: "On this day, I appoint Aki Ullis as the dedicatee of all my poems, past, present and future, and make her the sole literary executor of my life, (DATED & SIGNED) Dominic Ullis."

The morning after their wedding, on Plaza stationery, in an extravagant hand, he wrote while she dictated: "On this day, I promise you, Aki Ullis, that I am done with heroin. I make this covenant on pain of losing everything I hold most dear: You." She had read it through and asked him to date and sign it.

And yet, in his nod she'd instructed him to undo this solemn pledge. She told him what he must do if he wished to talk to her again. *Take more heroin. Accept heroin as your new god.* These were words she would never have uttered in life. It had not been her. He had conjured her ghost because he needed to see her. He needed to speak to her. Most of all he needed to hear her voice, because her voice was the single most irreplaceable part of her, unavailable in photographs or texts or signed undertakings. And so he had put the words into her mouth. It was a way of absolving himself and giving himself permission to fall back into the arms of heroin. Aki wasn't to blame. He was.

At six-thirty he went around the corner of Lucky's to a street-side teashop where half a dozen used Exide battery cases served as preferential seating. The day was beginning like any other day. The smog smelled of sulphur. Plastic smouldered on a dump by the railway tracks. A gang of children were picking through a mountain of garbage, hunting for metal, paper and glass. Men and women went to work, eager and unaware.

Danny wore a form-fitting black T-shirt that said, in white letters, IBO. He looked unusually fresh for the hour, as if he had had eight hours of uninterrupted slumber and no drugs whatsoever.

"Sir, you want to know something?" he said.

"Sure, Danny," said Ullis. "I don't see why not."

A boy in shorts and a khaki shirt put two glasses of milky tea on a stool in front of them.

"Cutting chai," said Danny. "Oh man."

The boy returned with a plate-sized fruit bun cut into quarters. Ullis took a sip of the sweet strong tea and considered the bun. It was almost tempting.

"You should know," said Danny, dunking the bun into his tea, "this is first time in my professional life I reach before the customer. Bro, you make me wait!"

"My apologies. Honestly. I know how unsettling this must be."

"We have a saying, 'Eze mbe si na nsogbu bu nke ya, ya jiri kworo ya n'azu.'"

Ullis took some of the bun and dipped it in the tea, and dropped most of it while attempting to transport said victual to his mouth. A mess of wet bread appeared between his feet. He took a sip of the tea, which went straight to his head – a most powerful and singular sugar rush.

He said, "I wonder if you'd care to give me a couple of grams of that good rock?"

"Already taken care of," said Danny, making to shake hands. He put two plastic bubbles in Ullis's palm and picked up his phone, which was buzzing.

"What does the Nigerian saying mean?"

"Is not Nigerian, is Igbo. Like me."

"Sorry, I knew that actually. Your shirt says so in sans serifs."

"Let's see. Let's see," said Danny, squinting at the sky while his phone continued to buzz. "Like this, the tortoise is happy to carry his own trouble on his own back. He don't wanna share no shit."

A breeze blew pages from a schoolbook against a long yellow dog stretched out in the gutter. The dog got up and cautiously approached. He sniffed at the fallen bun and looked at Ullis for permission, then dispatched the bread and licked his mouth clean and waited.

"A translation?" said Ullis, giving the dog a big piece of sugary buttered bun. This too vanished with a quick flick of the tongue.

"You must carry your own, uh, problem?"

"Burden," Ullis suggested.

"Yus, bro, that's it! You got to carry your own burden."

"And your own Bourdain," said Ullis, remembering the charming heroinated chef who had taken his life the same way as Aki, leaving his body to be found by a friend. And what of said friend? Forever traumatised, unable to remember important details of the event, he would blame himself, would find it impossible to believe in permanence of any kind, would develop acute claustrophobia and worse fear of flying, insomnia and hyper-vigilance, a love for reckless or self-destructive behaviour, and worst of all, he would carry this litany of maladies until the very end of his life.

Had he recited the litany aloud? Because Danny looked up from his phone and regarded Ullis with alarm as he texted a message, perhaps to his next client. Beside them, wage labourers were having breakfast before work. A steady stream of white-collar workers hurried past in the direction of the station. The dog settled down at their feet and went to sleep. Ullis put cash on Danny's seat and secreted the plastic cocaine bubbles in the inside pocket of his suit jacket. Like the self-sufficient tortoise he was happy to carry his own burden.

"I got to go sir, my next customer here," Danny said.

A black Skoda pulled up, freshly washed and gleaming in the mild morning sun. Music leaked from its windows, a droning squall fit for the king of a smoggy country on the last morning

of the last day of the world. Ullis took some comfort in its ferocity and volume, loud enough to drown out even the voices in his
head. Danny went around to the passenger's side and got in but
the car didn't move. Instead the tinted driver's window powered
down and a familiar voice rang out: "Domsky!"

It was Neel, starting the day with a purchase.

"Knowledge is powder and powder is knowledge," he said with
all the gravity he could muster. "Get in!"

CHAPTER FOURTEEN

By way of greeting, Neel turned up the music, the buzz and drone of The Jesus and Mary Chain, disaffected white boys dressed all in black and gazing at their black leather boots; and the fuzz-box distortion was the correct soundtrack to the broken city's well-appointed suburban slums, the hutments rising three floors and more, the flat roofs crowded with satellite dishes and beach chairs and split air conditioning units.

Danny's phone lit up, and he checked the screen and texted a fast reply. He settled into the front seat and tried to relax, but how do you relax when the music is designed to stress you out?

"Why you playing this hard stuff," he shouted. "You don't have hip-hop, man, or some groove sexy tunes?"

"No," said Neel. "I do not have hip-hop and I do not have sexy."

"Thank you," said Ullis.

"I can't help you boys if you don't wanna be help," said Danny.

"I don't wanna be helped," said Neel.

"Okay! Let we do business?"

In the front of the car money was exchanged for goods, and Danny's phone buzzed and lit up again and proved, if any proof was needed, that he was the hardest-working man in the narco business.

"How come Indian peoples always so angry all the time," he said when he had checked his messages, "like old Indian peoples, angry all day long. How come that?"

"I'm not angry," said Neel.

"No, not you," said Danny. "The music you playing is angry but you okay, bru. Some Indians not okay. Bit racist, yeah? Old and racist."

"Well, Danny," said Neel, nodding sagely, "there's nothing venerable about the aged. They're assholes too, just older."

With a series of stops and starts, the big Skoda negotiated the first of the day's traffic jams. They were stuck behind a motorcycle on which a family of five had managed precariously to fit, the father the only one with a helmet. To the right: a lake enclosed by a high fence that had not prevented a tide of litter from washing up against the banks. On the far side of the lake a snowy S shape moved against the dirty water. An egret. Lost, surely? The second Ullis had seen in as many days. Was it egret season as well as regret season?

"I'm breaking loose on this moonlit night," sang Neel joyously, only slightly out of tune, his round sunglasses moving with the beat. "I cut the road like a sharpened knife."

In a hurry to get out of the crush of cars, he made a hard left towards Waterfield Road. A traffic cop stepped out from behind a truck to flag them down. What was a cop doing on duty so early in the day?

"Fuck oh fuck shit," said Danny.

"Everything is cool, Dan man," said Neel. "Don't freak out now. They're trained to smell fear."

"Yus shit fuck," said Danny, rigid in his seat.

The cop wore Ray-Bans and a Village People moustache. The creases in his khaki trousers cut the road like a sharpened knife. There was an unmistakable spring to his step as he walked to the car.

"Driver's licence, dena," he said.

"But what did I do?" said Neel.

The cop told him he'd made the turn after the light changed. Neel took off his sunglasses and fixed the man with a look of deep disappointment. He made a long explanation that Ullis could not follow because the music was too loud. At the end of it, the cop leaned in to look at the others in the car, Ullis in the back seat and Danny in front, visibly sweating and hurriedly putting on his seat belt. The three men looked as if they'd been up all night, driving around and head-banging to the insane music that Neel refused to turn down.

"Driver's licence, dena," the cop said again.

Reluctantly, as if he could not believe the injustice of it, Neel pulled out of his hip pocket an old-fashioned buttoned purse stuffed full of documents and photographs. Kya yaar, he told the cop, shaking his head as he went through the wallet's many compartments, examining each one. Finally he extracted not the laminated card most people carried but an old licence the city no longer issued, an ancient booklet, its binding come apart with age. Now he began to remove sections and display them on the dashboard, glacially, with infinite patience, one frayed page at a time. He began to stack them in order. Kya yaar, he said again. From time to time he would nod along to the music, Jesus and Mary loud enough to rattle the windows.

The lights had changed and the traffic cop stood in the street, regretfully noting the cars that went past. He should have been out there flagging down drivers and earning his morning chai paani. He looked at his watch: 8.10. Soon the morning shift would be over, the lucky morning shift gone and nothing to show for his trouble.

"It is a bit of an imposition to be pulled over so early in the morning when a man is out looking for some breakfast," said Neel, rearranging the pages of his licence.

"Hindi?" said the cop.

"Nahi," said Neel. "English."

"Marathi," said the cop.

"Nahi," said Neel. "Sorry."

The cop had hoped for an early and auspicious start. He had hoped for a decent boni to get the good luck going. He wasn't any more superstitious than the next public servant, but it was the first transaction of the day and it looked like the day was going to hell. Gone! Gone to hell.

The lights changed again and the cars streamed past.

When Neel finally arranged the pages of the licence in the correct order, he held it out to the cop, who did not want to look at it, much less touch it.

"Chaliye, nikal," he said, waving them on.

"Ek minute, yaar," Neel said. Considering all the labour that had gone into finding his licence and assembling it, he was in no hurry now to leave. "Take a look, boss. Come on."

"Nahi," said the cop. "You can go."

"Yaar," said Neel. "This licence is old but gold. Why don't you examine it?"

"Bro, come on," said Danny.

"Chaliye," the cop said, trying not to beg. "Please to go."

Reluctantly, as if it was the last thing he wanted to do, Neel put the car in gear and drove slowly down the street.

Danny asked to be dropped off at the next corner and left without a word, and in minutes he was lost in the crowd of pedestrians, a sweaty guy in a beanie crossing the street with his head down, psychedelic fanny pack glowing dully in the light.

Ullis moved to the front, and turned the volume low on Jesus and Mary and the eternal infernal Chain.

"Just so we can hear each other without shouting," he said.

"Yeah, okay," said Neel, edging back into the traffic. Behind them was an ambulance, siren blasting, caught in the jam like everybody else. "This city, sometimes I wonder why I live here. I think I've earned the right to move. The Mary Chain turned up high? Insulation. Coke first thing in the morning? Insulation."

"You say insulation, I say fortification."

"I mean, look at this. It feels like the city's unravelling and I am too, constantly, you know?"

"I think so," said Ullis. "Where are we going?"

"Let's stop by the shop. Don't forget, there's nobody there for an hour at least. We have time for proper insulation."

They drove towards the sea through winding familiar streets, old houses made yellow by the morning sun. Neel parked on an incline, the hilly street empty at this hour. He unlocked the cafe's iron gates, and they circled past the shaded outdoor area to the cool rooms inside where he switched on lights and air conditioning. On a table hidden from the street they laid out the fruits of their labour, the smeared white lines that Ullis snorted and Neel rubbed into his gums.

"Deviated septum, man," he said, quietly. "Deviant, too."

Neel was a slow and steady user, a connoisseur of the maintenance dose, who liked to build his high over the course of a long evening at the Bandra Gym, or lunch on the balcony of a bar overlooking Juhu Beach, and as the afternoon faded into evening the whisky would soften his face and voice, and a younger man would emerge, a melancholic witness, friendly and stricken.

By the time the staff began to arrive, all incriminating material had been put away. They were bright-eyed coffee-drinkers, old friends deep in conversation.

"Listen," said Neel, "I want to ask you something."

A boy put a jug of green juice and two cups of espresso on a low table nearby.

"Not there," Neel told him. "Put it here," indicating the counter. "And where are the glasses for the juice?"

It was the first order of the morning and there was a system to this thing, to ensure its smooth operation. If Neel didn't oversee it, the system would fall apart in a day.

"He's new," said Neel when the waiter had gone. "Let me ask you something."

"Of course."

"You ever fantasise about doing a runner, like the French artist, take off to Tahiti and paint women and trees for the rest of your life? Trees and women and horses on the beach. I think about it off and on. But where are you going to go? Tahiti's full of traffic and plastic straws like everywhere else, probably."

"You could go somewhere war-torn, Afghanistan, say, or Somalia. That's one way to start over."

"How do we do it? Why? Live one life for the whole of our lives, sleep in the same bed every night, have sex with the same person, grow old with them."

"I wouldn't know," said Ullis, trying not to sound whiny.

"Sorry, sorry. I didn't realise how terrible that sounds. I'm so sorry about Aki."

"It's okay," said Ullis consolingly. "No. It's not okay. I don't know why I keep saying that. It will never be okay."

"There's something to be said for the old NA jungle sayings," said Neel. "Fake it to make it."

"Misery is an option," said Ullis.

"Sleazy does it."

212

"Hurt people hurt people."

"Ouch. Meeting makers make more money."

"Sit in the barber's chair long enough and you'll get a mullet," said Ullis, thinking of Sonu, his smoking companion of the morning.

"One day at a time, because the alternative is too horrific," said Neel, massaging his eyes.

They sat quietly for a while, the silence broken by a sudden barrage of honking on the street outside.

Neel said, "I'm going to head home in a bit, get a shower and some shut-eye."

"Darkness at noon. When will you quit this vampiric behaviour, young man?" said Ullis.

"Hopefully never. Except, when I see the kind of squares who do drugs these days, I don't want to go near the stuff. I want to clean up and take off to fucking Tahiti."

The waiter put a bowl of soup in front of a woman on a neighbouring table. The bowl had handles on both ends and across the rim in large capitals the word, SOUP. Ullis noticed that the coffee cups sported a similar legend: COFFEE.

"I've never understood the modern tendency to label objects with their function," said Ullis. "Where will it end? Houses labelled HOUSE and pets labelled PET? Just in case you get them mixed up."

"I'll be sure to mention it at the next board meeting."

"You have a board?"

"Of course I don't."

They downed their espressos and sat up a little straighter, as if they'd taken shots of wormwood absinthe. They downed their espressos and blinked at the day, a day like any other.

"And what," said Neel, putting down his cup, "are your plans for this fine Monday morning?"

"Is it Monday? Already? Makes an improvement on yesterday, at least. Sunday is a difficult day anywhere."

"The weekend is definitely over for some people. I can drive you somewhere if you like."

"Could you do me a favour?"

"Sure."

"A big favour."

Small pause. "Yes," said Neel bravely.

"Could you drop me to the airport?"

"That's not a big favour. Of course I can. Where are you headed?"

"Back home, I think."

"Where's that? Delhi?"

Ullis looked at his hands clasped on the table, and imagined folding her clothes and opening the drawers of her felt-topped desk and arranging her papers and books and collection of heart-shaped jade pendants. It would take days and weeks of sifting and tidying. It would give him something to do with his hands.

"Not sure if home is a city or a house or a person," he said. "Whatever helps you feel not alone, I suppose. It's time I went back. Her clothes are in the closet, trousers on the left, tops on the right, dresses in the middle. Everything neat and ordered, all her things all over the place, I'll never be alone."

Neel finished his juice. Ullis stared at his and marvelled at its greenness and evolved function in the world. He wondered that the glass did not say, JUICE.

"Will you get some closure?"

"I don't know if I'm in the market for it," said Ullis. What was it anyway, closure? A concept? A notion? Like *happily ever after*? He'd always thought of those things as natural mysteries akin to unicorns and double rainbows. He never expected actually to find them.

"So," said Neel with the air of a scholar-priest or a detective, "what are you in the market for?"

"Forgiveness would be nice."

"I hate sentences that begin with, my therapist told me," said Neel, "but my therapist told me that forgiving or not forgiving someone depends on how hard you want to be on yourself. When you forgive you're being easy on yourself."

"Well in that case I'm doomed, aren't I?"

At the security check, the uniformed officer in his smart beret asked Ullis to empty his pockets. The drugs were gone. In Neel's black Skoda with the black-tinted windows, parked at the airport lot, they finished the last of the cocaine he'd bought from Danny. In the airport bathroom he finished the last of the heroin. He hadn't wanted to share it with Neel, whose recovery was nothing if not shaky. When the security guy asked him to empty his pockets, Ullis placed on the counter his cash, a pen, credit and debit cards, his phone, his iPod, the passport photo of Aki, his boarding pass, and a business card folded into a square enclosing a suspicious whitish powder.

"Yeh kya hai?" asked the officer.

"Mera wife ki ashes," said Ullis. Then he remembered the Hindi word for ashes. "Raakh hai, mera wife ki."

The security officer examined the passenger's soiled white shirt and disreputable suit and rubber slippers, the red-veined eyes and the black shadows under them, the white stubble, the absence of a shoulder bag or laptop or any of the objects carried by other passengers. But none of these things made as much of an impression as his air of weariness, a childlike sense of aftermath that clung to him like the scent of sandalwood. Those *were* his wife's ashes in the card, folded clumsily and spilling on the counter. The officer had no doubt about it. He could see it on the man's face, the dazed expression permanent as a Maori tattoo. He stamped the boarding pass and let him through. The passenger tripped as he stepped off the platform. With a complex sequence of lunges and sidesteps he managed not to fall.

He wandered aimlessly around the airport. At a gift store, inspired by Ninja seth, he bought a pair of snowy white kurta-pyjamas. In the restroom, he shed his suit and shirt and stepped into the pyjamas and tied the knot at the waist. He transferred everything from the pockets of the jacket to the roomier pockets of the kurta. Dropping the suit into the trash, he looked at himself in the mirror. His reflection made him flinch and put on his sunglasses. He emerged from the facilities in the Indian colour of mourning.

Near the airport viewing gallery, he found a sports bar and ordered a large Jim Beam and a glass of lager. While he waited, he checked his phone for news of the American president. A video of his latest provocations would be just the insulation and fortification he needed. Instead he found his texts to Aki. He scrolled back and found the messages from her that he had read on the day of her death without absorbing a word. He hadn't looked at them since.

When his order arrived, he downed the Jim and took a sip of the beer and clicked on the first message: "I'm done. I'm going home. I love you; I'm sorry." He checked the date and time: 31 March, 11.32 p.m. It had been after she got home, which meant 'home' in the text was not a reference to the apartment at Defence Colony. She sent the second message half an hour later, on April 1 at 12.01 a.m., not long before she climbed the desk and attached a dupatta to the ceiling fan. It said: "Nobody is to blame; least of all you, my darling Dommie."

He had a sudden rush of memory. Her face when he brought her down, the change in the taste of her breath and the blood flowers under her skin, the roses she'd always disliked, hundreds of crushed roses on her cheeks and neck and forehead. He remembered their argument when he had almost crashed the car. When he went to her office to pick her up she wasn't there. Out with friends, the receptionist told him. She hadn't picked up her phone. He'd gone in search of her and still she wouldn't take his calls. He remembered when she finally called, late in the evening, the steel in her voice when she heard people laughing in the background, how abruptly she had hung up. The call was at about 11.15, just before she sent him the first text. When she sent him the final text he was almost home. It had been that close.

He remembered something she used to say in a teasing child-like monotone, "Nobody loves me." She had said it so often it became a refrain that he could not help but take personally. And he always responded in the same way, "I'm nobody." He thought of the note she left on her desk: "Nobody is to blame," on one side of a Post-it, and on the other, "I'm sorry." He knew why she had written it. Even at the last moment she had wanted to protect him from the police and from the accusations of strangers. Now, a handful of strangers at the bar stared as if he had just sprouted wings. What did they see? Dominic Ullis was doing something with his hands at last. He was trying to brush the wetness from his face.

He left his phone on the table to check on the flight, which should have begun boarding. He was flying Air India because it had business class, but the airline was widely unreliable. As if in confirmation of this well-known law, the information board said the flight was yet to arrive. He went back to the bar and replaced his tepid beer with another.

The last hit of H had left him level. It had cancelled out the cocaine and brought his over-stimulated over-sedated system back into a natural balance. But the Beam and the beer brought the heroin back, every grain of it brought back and enhanced. His eyes shut and his head tilted forward and he was back in the land of nod.

"Do you remember once," said Aki, "we were attending a lecture and I scribbled something in your notebook? It was a question I wanted to ask the speaker. You added a line or two. Do you remember?"

"I don't, no, or I think I do."

"What's the point if you don't remember these things?"

"Not much point at all, which may be the point."

"Stop being clever. This is me, your wife, you can be yourself."

"Unclever."

"If you wish. Anyway, after you added to my question, I wrote, *I love you. Please write something dirty for me.* Do you remember that?"

"Yes, I remember."

"No, you don't. You wrote: *When we get back to the room I'm going to lick you until you smile.*"

She laughed, a rare sound he had only heard twice or three times.

She said, "I don't think you should take heroin any more. It was never my idea. It isn't good for you and it isn't any good for me. It's time, Dommie. You should let me go."

He came to with a start and went to the board to check on the flight. The gate was closing. How? It had hardly opened. He hurried back to the bar and left money on the counter and ran to the departure gate, which of course was at the opposite end of the airport. As he ran he noticed other people running, and when he got to the gate he found a crowd of passengers convinced they had missed the flight. The indicator had gone from *Scheduled* to *Gate Closing* in minutes, though the flight had only just arrived. There was much shouting and confusion. Eventually, in his seat, he looked for his phone to switch it off. And that was when he realised he'd left it in the bar. He went to the front of the plane to talk to someone.

"Sorry, I've forgotten my phone," he said. "Do you think I could go back and get it?"

"It's not allowed," said the stewardess, an older woman with a well-earned air of unflappability. "Once you're aboard you can't leave. But let me check."

There was general consternation all around. It should be my name, General Consternation, Commander of the Chaos.

The stewardesses spoke to the captain, and the captain made a call, and a few minutes later someone from the ground staff arrived to escort him back to the bar.

See Dominic Ullis running through the terminal in his black flip-flops and white kurta-pyjamas, running awkwardly, followed by a man in a uniform. See him looking for the sports bar. There it is, and his phone is waiting at the counter! See him running back to the plane. See him hurrying to his seat, sweating and out of breath, his heart pounding, and someone in the front row is saying, "Did you find your phone?"

"Yes, thank you," he replied.

Two rows later, a woman in a suit and sunglasses, "Did you find your phone?"

"Thanks, yes," he said.

He got to his aisle seat and slipped in. His neighbour, a man wearing chunky gold jewellery, said, "Did you find your phone?"

"I did, thanks," said Ullis, "but how did you know I'd lost it?"

"The captain made an announcement," said his neighbour. "He apologised on your behalf for the delay. We're late by half an hour."

Ullis apologised on his own behalf. Soon the plane backed slowly out of the bay and turned into position for take-off. It taxied for a long time and stopped. For a long time nothing happened. Then very slowly it turned again and returned to the departure bay. The pilot made an announcement. "One of our passengers is having a minor problem with her heart. If there are any doctors on board, please contact the flight staff." A minor problem with the heart. Was there, could there be such a thing? No, there could not. It was a misnomer, a presidential misstatement. There was nothing minor about the heart and its problems. After what seemed like a prolonged delay, a wheelchair was brought on board and a woman taken out swaddled in blankets.

Ullis went to the bathroom and carefully unfolded the business card and placed it on the sink. Then he rolled up a note and snorted the last of his wife's ashes. It made him remorseful that he no longer had anything left of her. But she would live in his nasal passages and blood vessels and in each throbbing cell.

He would carry his own burden like the tortoise.

It came to him then that he had forgotten his phone and saved a woman's life. He had read Aki's texts at last, *I love you; I'm sorry*, and he had forgotten his phone. If he had not, if the woman had had a heart attack when the plane was in the air, she might not have survived. What was it that Aki had said? He who saves one life saves the world entire. He had been unable to save the life most precious to him, but he had saved a stranger. If this was possible, well then anything was possible. Even forgiveness. Even joy.